Kirk Camero... Cha...

By Mandy De Sandra

Julie

Believe in Chaos Magick

Mandy De Sandra

This is a work of fiction. Names, characters,
businesses, places, events and incidents are

Gonzo Gone Wild

1) Kirk Cameron & The Crocoduck of Chaos Magick

2) Gay Zombie Sluts in Key West

3) Duck Me in the Bass: An Autocorrect Anal Sext Adventure

4) City on Fire: A Novelette

5) The Haunting of the Paranormal Romance Awards

6) The Infinite Jest of Picking Porn Titles

Kirk Cameron & The Crocoduck of Chaos Magick

"Magick is the doorway through which we step into mystery, wildness, and immanence." Phil Hine

Myrtle Beach, South Carolina. Kirk Cameron's Camp Pray the Gay Away.

The boys sat on their blue beanbags. They were all in the 'Keep It Real, Say What You Feel Room'. The men behind the cameras twiddled their thumbs and wiped the sweat off their brows. The cameramen didn't mind, they were getting paid by the hour, but the boys on the beanbags had arrived days before the cameramen.

They were not allowed to talk to each other and they each had a chaperone watching them even when they went to the bathroom. Especially when they went to the bathroom. That was one of the first rules they learned at Camp Pray the Gay Away—no talking to other homosexuals, and only one man besides the chaperone in the bathroom.

Most of the boys followed the rules. They were raised good Christians and hoped they would learn to pray the gay away, but one boy felt differently. His name was Justin but said he wanted to be referred to as JJ and not be 'brainwashed by that Growing Pains asshole'.

Not only was JJ very proud to be gay, but he was also a practitioner of Chaos Magick. His first day at the camp he had to be reprimanded and even assigned a muzzle for trying to cast a spell on Kirk Cameron. This was not the first time JJ had tried to cast a spell on Cameron.

While the other boys were lusting after athletes and watching Sports Center, JJ was plotting to bring Cameron down with a Chaos Magick spell. JJ came from a family of good Christians who lived near the swaps and made him read Cameron's books religiously. JJ hated Kirk Cameron's books even more than he hated living in the Deep South.

He found hope and escape in a Facebook Chaos Sex Magick group. Not only did he find sexual fulfillment with the other young men in the group, but he also found spiritual purpose and strength. Through learning the teachings of Chaos Magick he saw how he could get his revenge on Cameron.

He wanted the former teenage heartthrob's lies to become real.

JJ decided to do his first spell. He printed screen shots of Magic Mike XXL characters, Kirk Cameron, and The Serenity Prayer with a picture of Jesus giving a beatific smile of hope.

He took them to the swamp, along with a tranquilizer rifle that his dad used on their pigs. He camped out and waited for the final ingredients: he needed a duck and a crocodile to complete his spell. The duck came shortly, it was an easy shot. It took another a good hour before he saw a young gator sunning itself. JJ shot the gator in the back and it passed out in the sun.

JJ used his gun to draw a pentagram in the dirt. He placed his gun on the ground and grabbed both animals. He put the duck on top of the crocodile in the center. This was not Satanism but the belief in Magick and Chaos becoming one to actualize his thoughts and desires. JJ wanted the duck and young gator to become one and go sexually attack Kirk Cameron.

The spell was not done, but JJ had all the right ingredients in one place. He took off his clothes and began masturbating to the pictures of Big Dick Richie and Kirk Cameron, as he focused all his energy into making his thoughts real.

He stroked hard and went faster. Moments before he reached climax he heard a voice say, "What in the hell! Get your hands off your penis and put them on your head."

Before he could take his hands away, JJ came hard.

The cum drops splashed onto the pictures of Kirk, Big Dick Richie, Jesus's Serenity Prayer, and the duck and crocodile. JJ heard the sound of a gun click and looked over to see a police officer pointing at him and said, "Don't move boy. Lord Jesus ... this ain't right. Oh my Lord. You're a damn faggot whacking it to a man of God. Blasphemy! And he is a friend of mine. Good man too, that Kirk Cameron. Brought me to the Lord ... holy hell ... you got your sperm on Jesus and Mr. Cameron ... you're of the devil!"

The cop spit out his Skoal chew and shook his head. He wiped the sweat off his furrowed brow and made the sign of the cross.

He took out his handcuffs and said, "Mr. Cameron's starting a camp for fags like you son. He has such a good heart, he might even open the doors for a demonic pervert like you."

Life had all gone downhill for JJ since he ejaculated onto those pictures and creatures. His spell had not come to fruition.

He was sitting in the beanbag circle with the other boys, seething with rage and frustration. He was hungry and hated being forced into silence by a muzzle. The beanbag had his ass falling asleep. He hated these stupid beanbags too. He hated that cop, his parents, and all the southern gay boys sitting next to him who bought into the bullshit of the camp.

His hatred only increased when Kirk Cameron's smiling face entered the 'Keep It Real, Say What You Feel Room'.

While JJ stared up at Cameron's face, looking like Hannibal Lector, all Kirk felt was love and compassion for the sick boy. Kirk Cameron wished the boy could see the truth of Christ. He knew that he had a spiritual sickness, which was like an AIDS of the soul.

Kirk reminded himself that he didn't hate gay people, just their behavior. He hated how Satan had seduced so many innocent young men through butthole pleasures. The holy war was tricky and Lucifer was trying to win by going through the back end.

Cameron understood he was fighting the good fight and would save one young soul at a time.

He looked at all the boys, besides the weird one in the muzzle, he could see their hunger for Christ. Cameron never once doubted God was working through him. He only wondered when the rewards would come.

When the camera crew noticed his entrance, the producers and cameramen clapped and cheered. Whether it was teen fangirls or his own crew, the sounds of praise were almost as good as God's love for Kirk Cameron.

"Hello everyone, today is a special day," he exclaimed happily. "Today is the first day of shooting. Before we get started on this exciting journey, I want to have some private words with Justin. It be quicker than the rapture."

The joke fell flat but the group of boys followed his words and went to the craft services table in the back to have whole grain turkey sandwiches, artesian waters, and special Swiss cheese slices.

Kirk sat on the beanbag to JJ's right and said, "Justin, I am going to have my assistant take off your mask. It's really important that you don't swear because curse words only make Satan stronger."

Kirk then looked over to a short statured thirty-something Hispanic man. He had a huge gap tooth and wore a gold cross. "Manuel, please take off Jonathan's Satan Silencer."

Manuel came over and made the sign of the cross and then kissed the cross that dangled above his chest. "Jesus loves you," he told JJ as he took off the muzzle. "Don't habla Devil. Habla Love."

Kirk nodded in agreement while Manuel unbuckled the strap behind JJ's neck and said, "Manuel was once a drug mule and a prostitute, but with Christ he changed his life and learned to read the Bible in English. These blessings can be yours. If you don't speak but listen with your heart."

JJ was free of the muzzle. He opened his mouth to stretch his jaw. He wanted to curse out Cameron but he knew if words came out, the muzzle would come back on.

He stayed silent and Cameron looked pleased and thought to himself, *the show is going to be a hit.* Yes, he wanted to cure gays at his camp but he wanted to do it on a hit Television Show.

Kirk Cameron had never been so bold and confident about a TV show. He had become discouraged when Fox News declined to produce "Kirk Cameron's Prayer Camp". Cameron felt he was on a mission from God to reach the secularists and didn't want to go back to Christian Television. He wanted a real platform where he could capture the same success he had with his sleeper hit Loveproof.

After praying about it, he read the liberal but enjoyable Christianity Today. He saw in the entertainment section the review of a new channel—NewsMax—a Fox News for real conservatives. Kirk could see the station really needed a hit, especially since their ratings showed that no one liked hard news about conservative subjects.

He had his agent pitch the show to NewsMax and they signed him and agreed to produce "Kirk Cameron's Prayer Camp" right away. The station saw that if they could get liberal outrage on Twitter as well as

Evangelical support—it would keep them in business for the next two years.

The docile JJ was a sign to Kirk that God would return him to greatness. It would be no walk through the shadow of death, but it would still be a challenge. JJ would be his greatest adversity but he knew God wouldn't let him down. God had only let him down once when he made the Left Behind Films. Kirk realized they were a test of faith and a realization that he belonged back on the small screen. While JJ forced himself to stay quiet, Kirk Cameron let himself dream.

"Ok guys, let's do this," Kirk said out loud. "Cameramen, please get set up. We are gonna get rapping."

They all walked over and joined him. Bob, a gay southern boy with a blond faux hawk looked at Kirk and asked, "Rapping? Like Lil' B the Based God?"

"Bob, now we all know there is only one true God and he is based in the Bible. No, we won't be doing rap music, but we will be keeping it real. We are going to go around the circle and everyone is going to say who they are and if they have accepted or want to accept Jesus Christ into their hearts ... once the cameras are rolling."

The cameramen fixed the lights and the boys squirmed under the spotlights.

Most of the boys had made sure to stay out of any limelight. They didn't want unwanted attention, though Bob and the boy next to him enjoyed using a flashlight while singing Taylor Swift songs to their mirror.

The lights were set and the main producer gave a thumbs up.

Kirk Cameron adjusted his posture and gave the same smile that got him on Tigerbeat for 3 weeks in a row in the 90's.

He looked into the camera. "Hello American and global viewers. You are going to be a part of an experience that these young men and I are going to share with you. It is a holy battle and this will be a proxy war ... with Satan. Yes, if you are looking for drama and high stakes programing, no matter what your belief, then you are on the right channel."

The young boys on the beanbags felt taken aback by the rhetoric. They also felt naked and scared. A few even wanted to stay at the camp forever, now that they had been outed as gay. They lived in places where they'd get beat up for being gay even if Jesus had supposedly cured them.

Kirk never thought about any potential consequences and carried on, "This show is not about me. It is about these brave boys who want to live a Godly life. Now I know some people will say what I am doing is an act of hate, but to make sure someone doesn't spend eternity in Hellfire. I think that is an act of love."

JJ coughed and had to keep himself from trying a Chaos Magick spell right then and there. He caught his breath and forced himself to nod in agreement.

Kirk smiled at him and turned his eyes back to the camera. "I started this camp to have a safe place for those who are confused and brainwashed. Mothers working. Twitter. Glee on Netflix and Hulu. These are only a few of the reasons these young men are confused. Well, we are going straighten them out through Christ, but first, we must meet these young men. Bob, we will start with you. Tell us how long you have struggled with your homosexuality and what is your relationship with Jesus Christ."

Bob looked nervous and lowered his face. He always was a shy boy and didn't talk to many people even at his community college in South Carolina. He kept his face down and spoke, "I'm Bob ..." he looked sideways at Kirk Cameron. "Is this like AA thing?"

"Just tell people who you are ... in less then thirty seconds," Cameron told him and then looked at the cameramen, "Edit that and this out too. Ok. Go on Bob."

Bob cleared his throat. "Well ... I'm Bob and I have homosexual feelings. I felt this way since I watched Dawson Creek reruns and had sexual feelings toward Pacey. I am a believer of Christ but I still ... I think about Pacey more then Jesus."

Kirk Cameron gave Bob a look of compassion. "Bob you are brave. I bet you didn't know that the creator of that show was Kevin Williamson. He is a homosexual who doesn't want anything to do with Christ. Dawson's Creek is part of 'gayifying' agenda of the Secular Humanist Left. Just look at Dawson, he was very gay. And his love interest Joey was very masculine and married a Scientologist in real life. Bob, let me tell you.

I met Kevin Williamson when I tried out for the film The Faculty as a science teacher. He gave that role instead to John Stewart. I could smell the evil on Kevin Williamson. He had the breath of Satan."

He smiled back at the camera and looked at the boy next to Bob. "Alight, Bill. Please go next."

The other three boys: Bill, Thomas, and Wilbert shared their experiences and their hopes. Their stories were similar: they felt isolated, loved Jesus, but none of them could pray away the gay. Even Kirk felt sadness for the boys. He remembered his non-Christ days and how the tabloids could be so cruel. But his compassion only went so far. It was JJ's turn.

Kirk Cameron tried to feel Christian love for the boy but deep down he felt no love or even trust for the kid. He saw that JJ wasn't battling Satan but trying to serve him with Dark Magic like his police friend said. Yet, he forced himself to remember that being a good Christian was hating the sin, not the sinner.

It would take time but he would help this Witch boy see the light. If he could help this boy overcome his gayness and Satanic spells, he could help anyone overcome their sin and find Christ.

"Ok, Justin. You're the last one. With respect and Christian goodwill please tell us about yourself."

A slight snarl appeared on JJ's face. He felt the numbness of his face muscles and didn't want to put the muzzle back on. He forced the emotion to leave his voice and stated, "Ok Kirk. Well, first, I actually go by JJ."

"Actually, nicknames are usually part of the gay lifestyle, so please start again," Kirk replied.

Bad memories came to JJ who remembered back to when he still used his birth name. He recalled when the teachers at middle school had shown the pictures he had doodled of a half-naked Criss Angel to the entire class. Even his gym teacher found one and screamed. "Justin is a faggot! Kick the cock sucker out of him."

When Justin got to high school he started going by JJ, not because of the gay agenda, but because he knew kids wanted to beat up any kid named Justin. These tough years made JJ look for solitude and find solace and empowerment on the Internet.

He found not only sexual but spiritual satisfaction in the Chaos Sex Magick Group on Facebook. Not only could he have cyber relations with other gay males in more sophisticated cities like Tampa, but he got turned on to a whole new spiritual worldview that gave him a renewed sense of hope.

With Chaos Magick he could finally be at peace with a world that runs on Chaos. If he worked with it instead of against it using Magickal rituals, then the universe would provide what he needed, including sweet vengeance on those who would wish to hurt him.

He was still no expert of Chaos Magick but he had the faith.

JJ accepted that the only way off this beanbag and away from this asshole Kirk Cameron was to finish that old spell that had been interrupted back in the swamps of South Carolina.

He looked at the camera and pictured his idol Criss Angel Mindfreak, staring back at him with his cool hair and mystic eyes. He focused on that vision and felt Chaos Magick and biology rise in his pants.

The other boys looked at his pants starting to rise, and he looked at the camera and declared, "I am JJ! And I am a Chaos Magician! I don't define my sexuality. I am Sex Magick. My boner will bring back yours Kirk Cameron, along with the Crocoduck. Along with even Jesus! I am now going to ejaculate in my pants and let Chaos reign!"

Kirk signaled to the producers for the cameras to stop rolling and screamed, "Manuel, stop him! Inject him!"

But it was too late. His prison-blue scrubs were stuck to his crotch.

Manuel could not stop JJ from ejaculating but he was able to inject his neck with a strong sedative. As JJ started to feel at peace, Kirk Cameron was silently repeating The Serenity Prayer to himself and was not feeling any.

The others boys stayed seated on their beanbags. One of the producers looked at Kirk and said, "What now Mr. Cameron? This definitely doesn't follow our baseline script."

Kirk wanted to yell at him; to even say blasphemous things at the producer, but he learned he should always pray first when anger rises. He learned this lesson well when he read the reviews of 'Saving Christmas' and went on Facebook to complain instead of praying—this caused even worse reviews of the film.

Kirk dug deep within himself and told them, "I'll be back in five minutes. I need to pray on it."

"OK, but I hope God is good at Improv!" the producer joked.

Kirk walked up to him and whispered, "Listen, I know you Jews are good with cameras. But remember only 144,000 of you will get into Heaven. Don't treat me like you treated Christ. The show will be great. There are blessings ... and there are blessings in disguise. Now excuse me ... sir."

Kirk stormed away to his own private dressing/make up room. He was happy that it had been built as he opened the door in the back of the 'Keep It Real, Say What You Feel Room'.

The budget didn't really cover it but some things didn't have a price. His dressing room was stocked with his still unfunded Christian Goldfish packet. It also had prayer books, pictures of Christ with His prayers, a mirror (for make up and spiritual reflection), and even his longtime photo-diary that went back to his 'Growing Pains' days.

He took a seat at the make up table and looked up at the picture to the side of the mirror. It was a popular picture of Jesus with a nice smile and the words of The Serenity Prayer.

Kirk looked into the contented face of Jesus and told the picture, "I'm not ready to pray yet my Lord. Give me a few moments of self-reflection."

Below the Jesus picture was his prized photo-diary. He picked it up and felt some of the tension leave him. It was worn out from all the years but still intact. Kirk had gotten it refurbished five times. It took three episodes of Growing Pain royalties to pay the bill.

Kirk opened up the front of his photo-diary and landed on page four. He saw his dear old friend Andrew Koeing who had played the role of Boner on 'Growing Pains'. Kirk even called him Boner off camera because he was a method actor. They were best friends on and off stage, but when Kirk found Jesus, Boner was left behind.

Kirk's acting and Boner's life had both met tragic ends—Kirk starred in the TV Show 'Way of The Master' and Boner took his own life.

Guilt would come to Kirk many nights concerning his old friend, but he would always pray and remember that Boner was destined to go to Hell, no matter what he would have said. He stared at the picture of Boner with longing and regret. He touched the dimple on Boner's smiling face with his ring finger.

Kirk took his finger off the picture and cupped his hands and prayed with his eyes closed. "Jesus. It's me. Kirk. I'm very stressed right now, Lord Jesus. I'm trying to show these boys that the only man they should love is You. But it is so hard. And that little jerk and his Satanic talk of Chaos Magick; I find it so unsettling and I feel the power of the Dark Lord. Please protect me True Lord and help me save that poor boy's soul ... I was once like him ...with Boner ... I don't want JJ to end up in Hell with Boner."

Kirk kept his eyes shut and stayed silent in reflection. He still felt the guilt of Boner but then he heard Boner's voice. "Kirk, I'm not in Hell. I'm right here bro. Look down, Seaver!"

Kirk opened his eyes and looked down to where he heard the voice. It came from the photo-diary. The picture of Boner was still two-dimensional but Boner was smiling and waving in the picture to Kirk.

"What the ... hell!" said Kirk startled and scared.

"Hey bro! It's me, Boner. I told you I'm not in Hell, Seaver," Boner said as he gave a two-dimensional thumbs up to his old friend Kirk Cameron.

"Oh my ... God."

Boner laughed and said, "There is no God buddy. Come on Seaver, don't give me that look."

"No God?" Kirk Cameron protested to the talking picture.

"Yo Seaver. You were you so wrong about that stuff. Let me tell you. Actually bro, Jesus can tell you."

"Jesus, my Lord and Savior? Boner this can't be real."

"But Kirk my son, it is," Another voice said, not from the photo-diary, but above it.

Chills washed over Cameron. He looked up and saw the picture of Serenity Prayer Jesus on his mirror. Like Boner, Jesus's blue eyes were blinking. His body was moving as he showed a different smile than in the original prayer picture. It was no longer one of serenity, but of pure joy. He waved at Kirk in the picture, and then waved hi to Picture Boner.

"No!" Kirk Cameron screamed. "You can't be my Lord Savior ... this ... this is Black Magic."

Picture Jesus's smiling face turned to thoughtful concern. "Yes and no Kirk Cameron. It is Magick. You see my son, I wasn't God, but I was the first Chaos Magician to walk the Earth. I am Jesus of Nazareth, not a god, or son of any god. There is no God."

"No!" Kirk protested. "There is a Heaven. A Hell. And a God. And you're Him. Jesus Christ, you're God."

"No my son," picture Jesus spoke. "There is only Energy, Magick and Chaos in the universe. The Magick called us."

"Ay yo, Seaver. He's right. There is no Hell, uh, or a Heaven even. Instead we're just like a Magick trick of energy. We come to you. We come to the most powerful energy that calls us. It's legit Seaver."

"No, it's not legit Boner!" Cameron screamed. "Lies! No, I am hallucinating. This is the work of the Devil! We are servants of Christ, not Chaos, Magic, and nothingness!"

Boner looked hurt and said, "You and me, we had Sex Magick that one time Seaver."

"So did I and Judas," said Jesus and winked.

"No more!" Cameron screamed and closed the book and threw it at the mirror. It broke the mirror as picture Jesus fell onto floor and wept.

Kirk ran out of the make-up room back into the 'Keep It Real, Say What You Feel Room' with the boys and the camera crew. Except for a drooling JJ sliding off his beanbag, they were all standing by the craft services table. The assortment of cheese and crackers were spread out and the boys and crew were enjoying them.

Cameron looked at the table of cheese and remembered he'd taken a few bites out of both and wondered if the food was poisoned.

Magic isn't really real, Kirk thought. *Christ was God and that couldn't have been Boner or even Jesus. No, I need to be like the secularists and use the power of science.*

Kirk had taken biology in homeschool before he was saved. He remembered the Scientific Method and the best hypothesis he could come up with was that he was poisoned or drugged by Social Liberal Terrorists. He had read stuff about Liberal Terrorists wanting to do this on the Drudge Report. He thought they probably had researched Tigerbeat and learned about his love for Swiss cheese. What a bunch of Satanic bastards.

He saw one of the cameramen about to eat more of the Swiss cheese and said, "Don't! Don't eat any of that food. It's bad. I've read on the Internet about how Liberal Terrorists want to poison social conservatives with hallucinogens. Stop! Put down that cheese."

The cameraman shrugged and said, "I've been eating this cheese for days. I'm fine. This is some darn good cheese, Mr. Cameron."

The other cameraman kept his hands in his pockets and said, "Maybe you should eat some more cheese or have some water, Mr. Cameron. You look a little pale."

Kirk walked to the table to inspect the cheese himself. He wasn't crazy. He was a Christian. He would see for himself if the cheese was drugged.

He reached the table and put his face to the cheese expecting a drug smell, but the smell was delicious and normal. He was about to lift his face up, but the holes of two slices of the Swiss Cheese shifted and contorted into the faces of Jesus and Boner Stabone.

"Hey Seaver, who moved my cheese. Ha bro!" Boner Cheese Stabone said.

"I love being cheese more than wafers and wine my Son," Jesus Cheese said to Kirk.

"My God!" Cameron screamed.

"It's Jesus and that Italian fella who was your friend on that show ... and ... they are ... talking cheese! What the fuck!" The freaked out cameraman said.

The other cameraman fainted and collapsed to the floor.

Cheese Jesus smiled and said, "Take my body. It's low in fat."

The Cameraman watched the holes in Cheese Jesus expand in width and length. He became a full body of cheese, including long skinny strands of delicious goat cheese for hair that fell down to his shoulders. He wore a flowing robe of delicious provolone holey cheese that hovered above the ground.

Boner Cheese split into separate cheese parts. It was the same number of all the conscious men standing.

The multiple Cheese Boners said in unison, "Ay yo guys. Have a bite of me. I taste better than Mrs. Seaver's meatloaf."

The cheeses jumped off the serving table. They dropped themselves into all the men's mouths and forced themselves down their throats. Miguel tried to avoid the demonic cheese but it squeezed itself through the gap in his front teeth.

Kirk Cameron and JJ were the only men free of Cheese Boners digesting in their bodies.

Cheese Jesus waved his large cheese hands 'hello' to Kirk and said, "Boner told me stories when he crossed over. I comforted him when he reached death. I do that for special souls. They are always looking for me when they cross into death. He told me his ... sins...his time with you, Kirk."

Kirk wanted to cry. His Lord and Savior smelled and looked delicious, but he brought up dark and erotic skeletons from his past. He looked away from Cheese Jesus and saw all the other bodies except for JJ's morphing into the same body shape.

They all became standing Boners.

The Boners smiled at each other and began getting semi-erections. They looked at Kirk and said in unison, "Remember when we finished Episode 10 Dirt Bike. We made sundaes and watched each-other while we touched ourselves. Let's do that with Cheese and Jesus."

The Boners stood tall with pride, all having the same sized erections. They looked at Cheese Jesus and he shook his head 'no'. Each Boner turned away from Kirk

Cameron and paired up with another Boner as they began kissing and fondling their clones.

Kirk watched them and felt the old feelings return. The ones he once asked Jesus to take away. But Jesus was a six-foot piece of sexy cheese.

Cheese Jesus reached his hand out and said, "Kirk my son, I know you thought I took your pain away before. But this time I will do it through my flesh."

Cheese Jesus walked closer to Cameron and continued, "I shall comfort you. This is my body, do with it what Thou Wilt."

Kirk smelled the intoxicating aroma of Cheese Jesus. He tried so hard to be good. So hard to prove his love of Christ, but here he was with his God as his most favorite food.

He nibbled on the ear of Cheese Jesus and said, "You taste so good. Is it really you, Jesus? You're Cheese, not God?"

"Yes my son. I never was God but I was always real," Jesus answered as he showed him the hole in his Swiss cheese hand. "I still have my wounds in this body, fill them up my son. Eat me. Stick me."

Kirk Cameron had fantasized about being raptured by Jesus; taken to Heaven in his Lord and Savior's strong arms and holey hands. Cheese Jesus grabbed Kirk Cameron's belt and took off his wrinkle-free khakis. His cheese fingers didn't break but they left delicious fingerprints on Kirk's black belt.

While the Boners kissed, Kirk shed a tear. His feelings overpowered him as he put his erect cock into the hole in Jesus's hand. Kirk had mediated about the pain in Christ's hands when he was dying on the cross, but his cock felt pleasure as he fucked the hole-hand back and forth.

The hole in Christ's hand was the perfect size. It was the old wound from dying on the cross that mixed with his body being Swiss cheese. The cheese gave a texture that touched all the right spots on Kirk's cock.

Cheese Jesus lifted up his other hand and held it out to high-five Kirk, "We are still pals, buddy. I'll take the pain so you can feel love in the heart that lives in your pants. I feel your pain and disappointment. But Chaos Magick can make you feel better then any false God. Oh yes Kirk, let your rage out on me like Judas did."

Kirk cried harder. He pounded the cheese-nail-hole hand of Jesus. His dick went through it, in and out, like when he and Boner used to play 'put your pee-pee through the TP hole'.

It brought Cameron to pleasures he couldn't experience with wife, but the pain of losing his faith was even stronger and he screamed, "No! I loved God. I loved my faith and I see it was all lies. The fucking nerds who played Magic the Gathering knew the truth about life. Satanic nerds! Nothing matters!"

The Boners stopped kissing and all eight of them looked at Cheese Jesus hand-fucking Cameron and said, "This is what I knew after the show bro. Nothing matters, man: It's Chaos, Seaver, and when you cross over you're just part of it. You've got to turn that Chaos into Magick."

Jesus took his hand away and said, "He is right my son, Kirk. I do not do miracles from God but I can perform Magick through Chaos of the Dead. The Magick your student JJ used has brought not only us, but a friend. He is at the door."

The Boners ran to the front door of the 'Keep It Real, Say What You Feel Room' as JJ started to gain consciousness.

JJ yawned and looked at the open door. His eyes widened when he saw what was walking inside and exclaimed, "It IS real," and passed out again.

"Yeah Kirk," Boner said as the creature waddled into the room, "It's a Crocoduck bro! And it is yours to play with!"

Kirk Cameron's mouth dropped and he fell to the knees. The Crocoduck that he had used to refute evolution was now in the room crocowaddling toward him.

It looked at Kirk and its wings flapped with glee. The green-scaled skin glistened while its feathers looked regal. Its 12-inch jaw of teeth showed a long smile of lust. Its Crocoduck cock was the same length.

The Crocoduck darted toward the kneeling, shocked, and open-mouthed Kirk Cameron. Kirk didn't close his mouth in time and took in nine inches of the Crocoduck. It squealed with delight while flapping its wings. The Boners followed the Crocoduck's lead but went into the 69 position. They sucked one another, mirroring each other, looking like a funhouse of fellatio.

Jesus smiled and looked down at Cameron full of Crocoduck cock. "My disciples said cheese made them blocked, but I will show you Kirk, that the right kind of cheese can open a man up."

Jesus took off his white robe of cheese and showed off his erection. His cock was average sized but it was a combo of exotic and exquisite cheeses. "I was born in Israel, but my cock is Moroccan, Greek, and French."

Kirk could barely hear Jesus as he continued fellating the Crocoduck. The creature of Chaos Magick was quack-moaning in ecstasy. Kirk was amazed at his deep throating ability. He once competed in a Christian Celebrity hot dog eating contest but lost to Stephen Baldwin—today was a different day.

Without a god to judge him, sucking a Crocoduck was not a sin, but a celebration of life. Kirk remembered Alan Thicke talking on the Growing Pains set about a Russian author who used a line, "Without God, everything is permissible."

The quote gave Kirk an existential crisis. The only thing that silenced that ache was accepting Jesus into his heart, but today that ache had returned and all was permissible.

Jesus spread apart Kirk's butt cheeks and put his cheesy dick deep in Cameron's asshole.

The 69ing Boners stopped sucking each other's cocks and followed the lead of Cheese Jesus.

They started fucking each other's asses and all of them looked at Jesus and said, "Yeah Jesus. I was back there back in the day. Seaver's got one sweet ass."

"It is better then Judas's and that redhead wasn't loyal but he could take a cock in the ass... oh yes Kirk. That feels so good. I have brought you real ecstasy and Magick. Heaven is here on Earth. Boners, bring that boy on the beanbag over here. It is time for some real Chaos Magick."

The Boners all got up and picked up a sedated and drooling JJ. They brought him over to Cheese Jesus. He stopped fucking Cameron in the ass to pet the Crocoduck.

"He's adorable," Jesus said. "God did not make this creature. Magick and Chaos did. It is time for you Kirk to be at one with Chaos Magick. The boy JJ, he has shown us the power of Chaos Magick. He performed it on you and summoned Boner, the Crocoduck, and I—a false God. It is time for you to claim your power back and worship the true God of Chaos. All is permissible. You can do anything Kirk. Anything. What did you want to do when JJ badmouthed you? You wanted to bring down Wrath and Chaos. Didn't you?"

"Yes, but good Christians don't do that but, now ..." Kirk said, as he looked down with shame struggling to accept and embrace Chaos Magick Cheese Jesus.

"Now! You know the truth, my son. I am Chaos Magick Cheese Jesus and through me all desires can be met. Pleasure yourself, Kirk, while strangling the boy to death. He practiced Magick to destroy you. Do the same to him and let Chaos Reign!"

Kirk looked into the crazy eyes of Jesus and saw the truth of Chaos Magick. He fixed his gaze back on JJ and felt all of his rage. He was the one that brought all this madness to him. He brought the Magick and showed him the horrible truth of Jesus and life.

JJ deserved to pay the price for the truth he taught to him. To know anything was permissible did not give Kirk Cameron freedom; it only caused him existential pain and he wanted to take it out on JJ.

The Boners went back to having sex with themselves and Kirk felt his erection swell with rage. It hardened, watching his first love, Boner, making love to himself.

"Make Magick Kirk," Jesus said. "Let go of the Divine Order you thought life was and be one with the Chaos and Do What Thou Wilt."

Kirk didn't pray or reflect. He let his emotions rule him and took his left hand and wrapped his fingers around his cock. He took his right hand, leaned into JJ, and started choking him.

"Life. Death. God. Heaven. Or Hell. None of it is real. None of it matters! I am at one with Chaos and Magick!" Kirk Cameron screamed.

Jesus smiled and so did the Boners watching him, but JJ's eyes shot open in terror. The drug had worn off and his survival instincts took over. He reached up with both hands and used all his strength to strangle Kirk Cameron back.

Cheese Jesus was pleased and aroused. He put his hard cheese dick back into Cameron's anus and held him down so both boys could continue choking and stroking.

Life was leaving both, but their grips became locked and neither man could let go as Cameron was close to cumming.

His last breath came and so did he, as semen landed on the face of a dead JJ.

Cameron awoke to see he was still in his camp but it smelled differently. The Boners and Cheese Jesus were there but JJ was not.

Kirk expected to feel pain in his throat but it wasn't there and he screamed, "Where is JJ? What the hell happened?"

Cheese Jesus smiled at Kirk and said, "He is not with us. He is above. I should have had him too but that is OK. I feel fine about it ... my son, HAHA. I got who I really desired. I got you, Kirk."

"Yeah, Seaver. This place blows hard, but it will be better with you here buddy."

"What is here? Why does it smell so weird, and why do I feel so hollow?" Cameron asked.

"Because you're dead, Kirk Cameron." Cheese Jesus said.

Cameron was no longer under the spell of Chaos Magick. It was not magical being dead. He felt a void and an emptiness in his chest.

Boner put his hand on Kirk's chest and said, "Ay Seaver, you'll get used to that empty feeling. You'll get used to the pain. But before you come with us, you get to meet Him.

"Who and where? I thought we were ... energy that stays on Earth?" asked Kirk Cameron, who was feeling worse with each passing second.

"You won't be able to go to Heaven with me, my Fallen Son," said a voice that sounded heavenly behind him; the voice wasn't erotic but it filled Kirk with an even greater pleasure.

Kirk turned around and saw it was another Jesus that wasn't made of Cheese but beamed with Love and Divine Light.

"Jesus!" Kirk exclaimed.

"Yes it is I. I am here and I AM real. You found my Love once, but for your last moments on Earth you forgot Me. Now, I must say goodbye to you my Son. You can't come with me to Heaven. You will go with Satan to Hell. I love you Kirk Cameron and it breaks my Heart to say goodbye."

The real Jesus disappeared into the air and the cheese of the other Jesus started melting away as the Boners morphed into one body.

The cheese all melted off of Jesus's body. Under all the melting cheese was a red burnt body of greater bulk. The cheesy Jesus face melted away and contorted into one of violence and hate. Two horns poked out its skull.

"Satan!" Screamed Kirk and wanted to cry but no tears came out.

"Yes, it was me along, Cameron HAHAHAH. I have wanted your soul and I got it. Magick and Chaos. HA, what nonsense. The world is ordered and full of choices. You chose wrong and your soul will be punished."

"No! Jesus come back! Satan tricked me. Please Jesus! Forgive me," Kirk pleaded.

"It's too late. Hell awaits," Satan proclaimed.

"Sorry Kirk," Boner said, "but I didn't want to be sex meat anymore ... at least we will be together Kirk, just like on Growing Pains."

"Silence Boner!" Satan screamed. "And no! You and Kirk will not be together."

"No please, Satan! I don't want to be sex meat!" Kirk screamed.

Satan look displeased. "My Demon Child needs love and food. You were the only one who said his name. The son I have loved since the early days of Earth's evolution. No one knew of my son, but you Kirk Cameron, you had the imagination to know he existed."

"What name? No, Satan. I don't know anything, please let me go," Kirk pleaded.

"You don't know that Angels raped the animals. That is why God sent me and the rest of us here. I was the Angel who had a Son with a mutated crocodile duck. My son is a Crocoduck! And he is lonely and hungry in Hell. I'll show you!" Satan said.

Fire engulfed the room and Hell's infinite sea of flame torture engulfed and destroyed the no longer existing 'Keep It Real, Say What You Feel' room. The mirage was gone and all that was left was Hellfire.

The Fire itself hurt more than anything Kirk Cameron had ever encountered on Earth. Hell was very real and he would give anything to redo his life. He closed his eyes and tried to pretend it was all a dream.

The ground started to shake and Satan laughed and told Cameron, "I can read your thoughts. No, you can't go back. You have a place here," Satan paused and smiled at his favorite sight in Hell. "Oh goody, my son is here. Who you met before was just an illusion. Here is the real thing. OPEN YOUR EYES KIRK CAMERON!"

Kirk's eyes opened to see a Crocoduck the size of a small mountain. The Crocoduck looked down at Cameron and licked his face.

Kirk screamed but Satan said, "Don't worry Mr. Cameron. That is not how he eats his food and makes love. He doesn't use his mouth."

Before Cameron could shiver out a word the Crocoduck turned around, stuck up its feathery tail, opened up his anus, and dropped it down around Kirk's whole body.

The Crocoduck's anus took Kirk right up into itself and Satan walked to his beloved Son. He gave him a kiss on his tail and said to Cameron dangling from the Crocoduck's anus, "He absorbs the juices of your soul daily and it sustains him for Eternity. It is much more painful than the Hellfire, Kirk Cameron."

Kirk felt the pain of the process, like he was drowning in a pool of hydrochloric acid. He let out the loudest scream but it only made the pain worse.

The Crocoduck smiled and absorbed more of Cameron's soul.

Satan patted his son on the back and told Cameron, "He loves when you scream. The vocal vibrations make him feel so good."

Gay Zombie Sluts in Key West

Since the zombies have been washing up on shore, I've been stuck with this horny old queen in his stupid storm-shuttered bungalow. He won't even run out of Viagra until a month from now, and all he wants to do is fuck my Twink hotness.
#ImboredasBritneys2007Hairstylist

If I knew the zombie apocalypse was going to happen last weekend, I would have gone clubbing in South Beach and gone out with a bang instead of being stuck with this creepy old queen down in his Key West 70's pornshoot villa...but he has coke that's even better than Lady Gaga's first album. #PokerfaceBitch

Before the zombies came, we were partying like A-list bitches and I let him do whatever he wanted as long as the coke kept coming. #TwinkiePrideDoingLines

He's a kinky old queen-fuck; I let him eat a piece of Key Lime pie off my dazzling cock and came in his old *Murder He Wrote* mouth.
#AngelaLansburyDeepThroat

He wiped cum and Stevia Meringue pie off his lips and said, "I love the taste of Stevia on your cock. You're just so fucking sexy. I want to take you to a special club. They don't let me in cause they are ageist assholes, but you're so beautiful they'll have to let us in."

#SteviaCreamPie

He then went on and blabbered some obvious boring truths about my beautiful toned size 28 Lucky Jeans wearing ass and how we are going to get into the most exclusive gay bar that didn't even let in Lance Bass in 2009. **#RocketCum**

We left his boring but high priced bodega with MSNBC saying something about a Cuban Virus Crisis. **#TheNewsIsForOldPeopleAndCatLadies**

Coked up and still full of cum I wanted to dance with these studs but the old queen kept blabbing about how these guys in the club all looked like Cuban Taylor Lautners'. **#TeamJacobBitch**

But when we got there and I was like **#Whatevs**

It was just lame and gross looking with red velvet cake covered ropes but there was at least a hot black stud guarding it. **#TayeDiggsOnRoids**

He looked me over but I didn't get the usual *fuck that twink bitch is hot eyes* and said, "**#WTF**, a straight bouncer? How 1997 **#BirthdayYear**"

The bouncer rolled his eyes said, "Listen you hashtag shit talking Twinkie, I only let 10's in and you are just an 8.7 and it's past your grandpa's bedtime, so go get some Vaseline and Stiff Nights and go home, bitches. *Club Wrecking Ball* only takes 10's. That is our tagline. Goodnight old yellers."

#OMG

I'm more pissed than a golden-showered bathhouse.

#TurkishGold

What was even more hurtful is I could hear the dopest club music and picture all those hot big studded cock boys dancing, probably doing bumps of quality coke off their cocks heads. **#ParliamentDicks**

And fuck that bouncer and his shitty-brown-need-an-eye-check-eyes; I am a fucking 9.3. I don't believe in plastic surgery or I'd be a ten.

#PhotoshopTheBlockIsHot

I was ready to curse that needs-Obamacare-to-get-his-eyes-checked-bouncer out when I saw the fucking grossest thing ever. It was a puny Cuban looking guy with wood stuck to his face; he looked like a Kardashian without make up. **#KhloeIsGross**

He was running toward us like a rabid dog you'd see in the film *City of God*.

#NetflixForeignFlixsAreTheBest

The bad-eyed bouncer stood still and took his big thick black anaconda arms and punched the gross wooden faced creature in its ugly face. #Sharkeisha

I thought he was out like Lohan on a Wednesday of a coke morning but that woodenheaded gross thing got back up and bit the hot black stud's right man breast.

#TittyTittyBangBang

The bouncer's nipple came off like a pepperoni falling off a greasy pizza and then the woodenhead thing looked at us. The wood was rotting and dropping from his head along with maggots falling off his scalp.

#HeadAndShoulders

#OMG I realized it was a zombie with terrible fashion sense and wanted me for my brains. #Irony

This nasty zombie growled at us and his red eyes clashed with the beige of the rotten wood. The music behind the door was loud but the zombie's growl was even louder #TeamMariah

He leapt at us but like my old days of being a male cheerleader I ducked just right and he missed trying to eat my *swanesque* neck. #BlackSwanBitch

My old queen finally did something useful and opened the club door and pushed the nasty wood-headed zombie into *Club Wrecking Ball*. I grabbed the pole holding the velvet rope dripping with blood and put it through the handle so that living raft of a thing wouldn't touch my fine filet mignon ass.
#BetterThanVealBitch

The zombie attacked the door and the growling stopped. A few seconds later we heard a lot hot man screams in pain. **#ILikeItRough**

The old queen grabbed my hand and said, "Holy shit! That was a fucking zombie. Let's go back to my place, I have hurricane shutters. They're solar powered. We'll be safe."

And we did and we have been here for over a week.
#HellOnEarthIsOldDickAndNoNetflix

We are now out of coke and out of food. We sucked each other's dicks just for nourishment; I am already tired of it, he has grey pubes too. It's gross.
#SilverSnakesOnAPlane

The news said the zombies came from Cuba—a CIA disease gone wrong. **#Whatevs**

The old queen and I are now spooning and I'm wishing for death. Ew, his skin is so gross, he leans in and kisses me on the neck. I shiver and feel hot water on my neck. Ugh, he sometimes likes to cum on my neck but then I hear him crying **#OldYeller**

I'm so not feeling old sad gross man, so not hot, but I let him talk, "I know you don't love me. None of you do. It's ok. I know I'm old, hideous, and a size 33, but we are going to die and I still never got into *Club Wrecking Ball*. I want to go into that club before we die."

Ugh, he's like if old lady's period could talk. I don't want to die with him.

#CryingQueensMakeMeWantToScream

I turn over and look at his old teary gross face, "Well, I don't want to die with you, and all the coke is gone. We should go there and see if they have more coke. **#ItchyNose**"

"Oh, my god, you little twink, will you stop with speaking in hashtags. Did all the cum you swallowed hurt your brain? Not only are their zombies outside but that club will be full of them, and they'll be hungry."

"Maybe for cum, that'd be kind of hot! **#CumSushi**"

"For brains! I don't want to be eaten to death."

"Oh yeah, they eat brains and nipples too. S&M is so suburban housewife #50ShadesOfBored"

The old Queen puts his hand on his undersized chin and scratches the puny thing like he is thinking about like important stuff or whatevs and says, "Wait, I have an idea. I bought us a gift, it would be perfect!"

"Oh, please tell me you have more coke #FloridaKilos!"

"No, even better, I bought us both leather gimp suits. That is why I asked for your size."

"It's so humid though #SweatyBalls and I am really a 29, don't tell anyone bitch. I get water weight #NotSmartWater"

"Oh, I should have listened to my shrink and not fucked young little pretty boys. You idiot. It doesn't matter if it is humid. We can walk outside and even get into that club. We can walk outside! We don't have to die here. The leather will protect us from being eaten!"

"Oh, it's like Halloween but with real zombies, a club out in South Beach did that last year. It was a total #BonerLisa"

"We could survive; get out of this house. Let's do this, I don't want to die here."

"#ASize29IsGonnaLookGoodOnThisBehind"

We take down the storm shutters and emerge from his tacky Pleasure Palace in our full body leather suits. I can't hear much and I smell like the lube section of a Sex Toy shop but the ocean air feels good on my nostrils. **#IStillNeedCoke**

The street looks like Drag Queen and Dyke Night at *The Parliament Club*. **#TheLWordSeasonThree**

#OMG there are a few gay zombies in the street, they still have great hair where their brains haven't been eaten. Oooh, one has nice pecs, oh, so does his friend they have beads from *The Bourbon Bar*. **#DeadSexyStuds**

The Old Queen grabs my hand and I hear a muzzled, "Don't run, they won't be able to break through the leather."

We keep walking as two of the zombie studs try to eat our brains but can't break through. Ooh, I am getting tag teamed and they are humping me. I can feel their big dead flaccid cocks against my leather ass. It's kind of hot. **#ViagraZombiesUpOnMe**

It feels good to be humped by such hotties but after a minute they stop and make these off-pitch zombie moans. **#LanaDelRayLiveOnSNL**

The other zombies see no one attacking us and leave us alone. **#OMG #50ShadesofSafety**

The old queen takes my hand again and we walk past a family of tourist zombies who have no legs and shoulders. Ugh, I hate children they even sound more annoying as zombies. **#HomeAlone2**

We pass the little freak family and make it back to *Club Wrecking Ball*. **#OMG** the door is still locked with the same fake gold pole my old queen put up. **#AtLeastThatStaysHard**

We stop and see are ourselves in the bulletproof glass window. Ugh, my body is so much better than his. **#DamnIamASize28Now**

He holds my hand and whispers in my ear with his old gross breath, "Whatever happens, I can die happy knowing I got into *Club Wrecking Ball*; let's go out with a bang at hottest club in the world."

"**#Whatevs**, I just want some coke." **#AllIWantToDoIsGetHighByTheBeach**

He takes the bar off and escorts me to go first into the club. **#BeautyBeforeAgeBitches**

We step in the club and the music is still pumping. **#GeneratorsStillGoingHaters** **#WeCantStopWontStop**

#**OMG**, they are playing the remix of *Royals*.
#**LoveThatSong**

But when we make it to the floor I see a group of zombies that are totally tens. #**SouthBeachDiet**

Even better, there are tons of eightballs on the floor. Some have blood on them but whatevs. I grab the bloody plastic bag, and do a quick bump off my hand. #**Scarface**

The zombies get closer and *Applause* by Lady Gaga comes on and I start grinding with the zombies. Ooh, they are humping me back and biting at my head, it feels good. #**BigMonsters**

The Old Queen sees a zombie in the corner with broken legs and I watch the creepy old fuck take out his below average penis. #**WhyHeIsDrivingALexus**

#**OMG!** That dirty scummy queen just put a condom on #**TrojanSilm** and is doing the broken legged hot zombie in the ass. #**KeyWestOz**

He is humping him harder and the zombie is screeching like a dubstep remix. #**Skrillex**

The old queen is really a lousy lay, way too jack-hammery. The other zombies come over. They are coming over, oh shit; they are going below, are they going to lick his balls? #**RedRover**

Oh shit! Gross! **#JohnWayneBobbit2014**

A zombie totally just bit his little dick off and now they're fighting over his little cock like dogs. He is bleeding to death on the floor. **#OMG** he is going to be a dickless zombie. **#AnotherExBoyfriend**

Shit, now I'm all alone...ugh.

#SeventhGradeLunch

Agh, I feel nauseous too, what the hell is wrong, something was off about the coke. My body ...

#EighthGradeLunch

Ugh, I just threw up in my mouth. **#FML**

Oh no, the coke...I got the blood in my nose.

#JusySayNoToZombieCoke

#DoubleFML I'm going to be a fucking zombie now.

You know what? **#Whatevs**

Living was kind of lame and at least I will be with the hot zombies. **#BetterThanBeingDead**

I look down at the old queen dying and remember how to get the headpiece off of the body suit. He's smart. Ooh, I bet his brains taste fucking good.

#FinallyGetSomeGetSomeGoodHead

Ooh, I want some brains now more than coke.

#YumBetterThanCum

I need it now. **#Feending**

I go to him, smile, take off my mask and lift up his mask as he begs for help and say,

"#INeedSomeBrains."

Duck Me in the Bass: An Autocorrect Anal Text Sex Adventure

Hey everyone. It's me Mandy. I have decided to be brave and just share some fun, intimate and lovelorn sexting between Trevor and I. This text exchange is real, full of passion and other things that his lawyer unfortunately is using in court.

Since my lawyer can't stop this evidence from getting out, I am going to put it in this anthology because that would make it fiction and inadmissible in court.

Thank you for enjoying this piece of "fiction" ;)
Now I don't have to go to jail.

Enjoy,
Mandy De Sandra

AT&T Text Message file recovered by NSA given to the 8th District Court between Mandy De Sandra and Trevor Clover

Trevor: God ducking dam, I want u. So bad! That ask of yours calls me...like sirens talking to Ulysses. I know u love that Glee Mythos. I want u like...a pizza. My cock is dough and your ass toll is the cheese.

Mandy: Im eating right now Trevor. U need to work on yr metaphors. U know I'm lactose and intolerant.

Trevor: Srry. My poetry preacher at the Community college tight class said the same thing. I luv that Im going back 2 my fist love of poetry. Toilet cleaning marketing has so much $ but not the xtc of writing a special poem. What r u eating? Are u imagining it is my cock?

Mandy: I'm having Chicken Salad.

Trevor: Is it as tasty as that asshole of URL??

Mandy: I cant lick my own past hole Trevor. It is good. I got it from Trade Off Joe.

Trevor: Ooh yeah, baby! It is so good. You don't even know. Ur past hole is better than Trader Jose. I love tossing your valid ;) Last night was so hot. U sat on my face 4 so long I coundnt breath for 2 whole minutes! I couldnt feel half of my face. #SoHot

Mandy: It was nice. Theres nothing wetter than getting my valid tossed on your yacht my sexy cock boy. So hungry 4 u and your touché cock.

Trevor: ☺ yeah, my luv... So what r u doing?

Mandy: Lunch break silly. But almost done.

Trevor: How bout we have a sexy snack...on the phone

Mandy: Trevor, uve sent me like 200 dock pics. I had to delete at least 50 to save on memory. And please no more memes involving you dick!

Trevor: I thought they were cool!

Mandy: They r ok. Just unoriginal.

Trevor: Whatevs...U want to text sex or just send me a pic of u lingering yr pussy?

Mandy: Trev, we've talked about this. I want u 2 b more imaginative, I want 2 feel like a teenager again. Be creative!

Trevor: This sounds hard...like my cock. Ur the smart one working for the Dept of Labor, u think of something. I am game whatexver it is

Mandy: ...Ok fine. Like usual I'll lead.

Trevor: I'm a marketer, not a leader ☺

Mandy: Ok! I got it.

Trevor: What??

Mandy: Why don't we play Double Anal Dare?

Trevor: Double Anal Dare? Like 2 dildos in my Aspen? I can't baby, I was barely able to take your cabbage white one.

Mandy: No. It's like truth or dare but if u don't tell the truth or do the dare u do have 2 put 2 things that I or u request up the ass.

Trevor: If I don't...what?

Mandy: You will never be inside my juicy pussy or tight asshole again. #Pussy&AssPower

Trevor: No! Don't say that bae! I wood die. Id kill myself. I rather be castrated then never peel that juicy country of yours.

Mandy: Well then, u either tell the truth, do the dare, or u have to go double anal of the projects of my choosing.
Trevor: Damn it bae, u got me so whipped. I am Cool Whip and u r a sexy French chef.

Mandy: Ugh the metaphors Trev, stop...I luv you in spite of them.

Trevor: I luv u 2. Alright. Ladies first ;) Truth or dare.

Mandy: OK. Dare ;)

Trevor: I dare you to masturbate that sexy Pusicfier of yrs and squirt on your chicken salad sandwich and then eat it. Baby, your pussy juices waste so good. It will make your Hater Joe bitchin salad.

Mandy: Ooh, I've never tasted my own squirt. Yummy

Trevor: It tastes like angel tears. I could brush my teeth and bathe in yr squirt juice.

Mandy: Alright...my fingers are in my wussy. I putt 2 n. I get wet imagining u eating me out and putting haughty things up my bass hole. Im still at my desk. They think Im eating lunch and I will finish soon. I am not wearing any thunder pears...I just licked my fingers and I can't wait how my Dell mistress pussy juice will taste on my Hater Jose Sandcastle

Trevor: U are so good with yr fingers! That's a lot of texting and fingering at once! Yes baby, squirt on your chicken salad!

Mandy: ... text me something sexy. You know what I like. I am getting close. Take me home Trevor. Frack me baby! Frack me with worms!

Trevor: Picture that my tongues have been cloned and they lick your bass hole, toes, and shaved country. My tongues lick at the same pace and motion until all the nerve endings join at once force until china shoots out a wave a surfer wishes he could ride.

Mandy: OMG! I DID IT! Jesus...we really have to find a way to clone tongues! That was hot. Ok luv. I am gonna see how it tastes.

Trevor: Send a pic!

Mandy: It makes it taste better! My puny juices goes well with the vegan manor haze. Here is a pic

(AT&T picture 89 SMS missing. Property of the 8th District Court of Washington, DC & the NSA)

Trevor: So hot, there is only one bite left!

Mandy: Not anymore. Ate it. So delish I'm full on chick salt and my pussy juice.

Trevor: Yum

Mandy: It is your turn now.

Trevor: Ok...dare.

Mandy: Shove that dildo u used on me up your ass. You know, the one you keep in the draw, that big black one next to lube. Wait you have two of them.

Trevor: For doublestuffing...but...its big!

Mandy: I know. Your dock looks so cute next it.

Trevor: No babe it is too big, I'll slap it against my cock and send it to u. I know u get off on SPH. I'll even do a measure compare.

Mandy: I already have pics of those. I want a pic of the niner up your toilet roll...u just don't have to go deep just the tip and take the pic.

Trevor: Its not length that scares me.

Mandy: Well u better do it r yr going to get two of those up that cute little ass of yrs Trevor. Or if u don't...say goodbye to this tight pus in boots.

Trevor: Never! No! Fine. I'll do it. Let me get the lube by the stapler

Mandy: Good boy, u know u worship these China lips.

Trevor: I do. I would rather be in prison than be forbidden to enter that yacht of yours.

Mandy: Hmm...interesting. Well that is for later. Right now u go get that lube and then send me the pic.

Trevor: Fine...

Mandy: Come on, I'm waiting...

Trevor: Here! It feels kind of good, but I can't physically fit two of these up there

(AT&T picture 90 SMS no longer available. Property of the 8th District Court of Washington, DC and the NSA)

Mandy: Ooh, it makes me want to finger myself again. I love seeing that big dildo up yr ass. U look like ur in pain and in pleasure. We have to watch Hellraiser 2 again.

Trevor: Maybe, I don't like the man with pins in his head.

Mandy: Pussy. ;) Alright, yr turn. Ask me truth or dare.

Trevor: Truth or Dare?

Mandy: Truth...Ask away.

Trevor: Ok, u got to hell the truth, or u got the two in trooper.

Mandy: Trevor I luv huge cocks in my pussy and in my ass, here... I am in the bathroom now and there is something or 'things' in my ass and its not brown but black.

(AT&T picture 237 SMS no longer available. Property of the 8th District Court of Washington, DC & the NSA)

Trevor: Holy shit, I didn't know it was possible. Bae, how did you fit two of those up your ass??

Mandy: Tantric yoga. We can go double anal some time. Your cock would feel so nice with one of the black dildos.

Trevor: U really can take some big cocks. That is so pot!

Mandy: Trevor I hide nothing from u and I will do anything. I fear nothing but my boss. So we will have to wrap this up in a little bit.

Trevor: I wanna wrap you in my cum. I want 2 make a cum blanket and cover u with it and keep you warm. Warm with my gum.

Mandy: That is sweet Trev.

Trevor: It's true.

Mandy: Ask me a truth or Dare.

Trevor: Actually, my dare was going to be to go double anal. So will u do truth?

Mandy: Ask me anything my Trevor?

Trevor: Do u love me, as much as I love you?

Mandy: Yes I do Trev. You asking me that makes me wonder if u love me as much as I love you. Dont my actions show it Trevor. I put those two dildos up my ass to show you I love you. Is not my hot brizallian waxed asshole filled to its capacity not an act of love?

Trevor: It was like watching a Shake sphere play.

Mandy: Ur my ass licking Romeo, but Romeo died. Show me r luv can live. Prove to me that you love me.

Trevor: Dare my love. Dare me 2 prove my love.

Mandy: Well, I actually want 2 have a threesome. With my cousin, she's even stopper than me. Ur by your desk right bae?

Trevor: With my dick in my handle and the door cocked.

Mandy: I dare u to go to your computer and keep holding that pesk dick.

Trevor: Always babe. Always ready, do you have a pic of your cousin?

Mandy: No but I have her G chat address and I dare u to show her yr dock. R you ready sexy?

Trevor: Yes, send it and I'll message her. I'll put my phone on voice text so u can hear her response in real time.

Mandy: She is like me and gets turns on by dildos up a sexy boy's ass toll. Ur gonna love her dig bits. And her pickles are nice pinky pointy ones. Real 2.

Trevor: Oh fuck that is so hot! Give me to me love!

Mandy: Put that dildo up your ass again. I want you to be able to cum right on the screen that will turn her on so much. Oh fuck I get so wet think about all 3 of us ducking! Me riding your dictionary while she sits on yr face and u lick that tweet squishy and past hole #Soaking

Trevor: Ok, hold on. I am ready for it again. I am nude except for the black socks you got me at JC Penny

Mandy: Go grab the matching black dildo and take another pic and I'll send you the G CHAT link to my cousin.

Trevor: Here my love! It feels better the second time around.

(AT&T picture 91 SMS not available. Property of the 8th Circuit Court of Washington, DC & the NSA)

Mandy: Oooh so sexy! Alright sexy boy, u earned this. Have yr dock hard and ready. She works at a dominatrix school. She teaches her sexy dom girls. U might get lucky and have other girls see u. Ooh maybe a 4some can happen!

Trevor: Send it! Im teddy.
Mandy: I let the school know…they are all excited. Ok it is Naughtyboys-Academy@gmail.com

Trevor: I am one naughty boy! I am about to g-chat them now…ok I can switching over to audio text

Mandy: They r expecting you.

Trevor: *"Hey sexy . . . oh god, there are kids. They are little boys . . . oh fuck . . . sorry, I mean . . ." "You disgusting pervert! How could you? The person said you were the football player RG3, not . . . my lord. Turn your eyes away children. Sir, I'm tracing you. I have your e-mail address. I am alerting the law you pedophile . . ." <voice ended> "Shit, shit, shit . . . what the fuck?!"*

Mandy: What the fuck Trevor is this prank?? Tell me you are ok??

Trevor: *"I am not okay! What the fuck Mandy?! That was a little boy's school! She was a teacher not a dominatrix. Did you give me the wrong school name?"*

Mandy: No. I did not . And URL a shitty liar, because you don't love me.

Trevor: *"This is not the time, you fucking bitch! They are probably reporting me to police. Fuck! I am so fucked!"*

Mandy: You should tell my sister instead. Maybe she will pay your bail.

Trevor: "You fucking cunt whore. You set me up!"

Mandy: U fucked my little sister. On your yacht of all places. She cold me everything. That is just a hotter and younger version of myself.

Trevor: "You are fucking psycho. You evil cunt bitch slut. Fuck you! I never loved you, just liked fucking you."

Mandy: Well, my sister doesnt love u r me. She is the evil cunt, but you my dear Trevor...u should be worried bout dour future cellmate. Flashing yourself to kids, Trevor, to the Naughtyboy Academy. So wrong. How could U. They will probably throw the cook at u Trev.

Trevor: "Fucking whore! No! No! No! NSA! Terrorist! Al-Qaeda! Jihad! Allah Hu Akbar! I want to bomb America! NSA NO, I don't mean that. Help me! I am just trying getting you hard workers of the NSA's attention. I love America! I hate terrorists. This woman is black mailing me. She loves terrorists. She dressed in burka once and had me pee on her. She set me up. Help me Homeland Security. Help me please. Prove my innocence."

Mandy: Oh, Trevor you are such a kidder. Our story is done. This is work of fiction you know. I am transcribing our texts for a *Strange Sex* anthology. Thank u, I think they will like this story.

Trevor: "What the fuck! No! This is not fiction! No, this is real. Please! I didn't know. I thought she'd be naughty S&M, not a British nanny with kindergarteners . . . fuck blee. . . I'm crying I can't even balk . . ."

Mandy: U r gonna be published Trevor. This is so exciting! U should be happy. I am.

Trevor: *"Fuck you, you cunt psycho whore! I need to turn this fucking text voice thing off . . ." <Voice Text Turned Off>*

Mandy: Aww Trevor. The cops will be there soon. Yes turn that off. It can be used for evidence, but this is a fiction story ;)

Trevor: I pope you fly! Duck you ducking bunt!"

Mandy: Ooooh that is a great last line for the story. Thanks Trevor ☺

City on Fire: A Novelette.

By Mandy De Sandra

Author's Note

Hey sexy people, though I think this story is very cool, it is not my own. I can't take credit for it but the author gave me full permission to publish it under my name. I usually write in Hemingway Blowjob Minimalist 3rd person prose, but this story was written in touching first person non-fiction. I knew that the reptilians were real as my boyfriend Trevor and I watch Ancient Aliens all the time, but I had no idea about how they were involved in publishing.

This brave old man sent me this story in word doc with instructions to publish it under my name. He said because of my success with *Kirk Cameron and The Crocoduck of Chaos Magick* this story would reach the right people. I found this story to be sexy, informative, and moving. For those asking if it is related to the 2 million dollar novel first time novel *City on Fire*, the answer is sort of; with the reptilians and the snake aliens—all stories are related.

Sincerely,
Mandy De Sandra

The city wasn't on fire, but it was ripe with cum of the reptilians.

The novel *City on Fire* has just been published. Authors keep complaining about how much money the writer received for the publication, but what they don't know is that the Illuminati lizard people are behind this novel of lies.

They paid the author Garth Risk Hallberg all that money because the Big 5 publishing companies are run by lizard people who don't want you to know the real truth; the truth of what really happened during the blackout of 1977.

I know the truth, because I was there during the blackout. The lizard people's cum didn't erase my memory like all the others.

Yes, the lizard people Illuminati reptilian aliens are very real, but what you don't know is that they bukkaked all over New York City during the blackout. Their semen erases your memory and your sense of self. They make humans act in whatever ways they want. The reptilians have gone from planet to planet to dominate and control other species with their semen and their stories.

It was the reptilians that invented 'the book' on their planet, and they are still using literature to control us.

The reptilians left their home planet 200,000 years ago and their spacecraft landed in the place we now call New York City. The reptilians claimed the land and ejaculated upon on all of the species—the creation story of the Bible is partially true; the reptilians took control of their Eden in 7 days. They can't reproduce but they can control almost anything through their cum. Anything but their rivals—the snake alien people that fell to earth too—but they fell in the Amazon.

The snake aliens had been at war with the reptilians for eons but in their battle, they were trapped in the Amazon while the reptilians conquered the rest of the globe.

The Amazon snake people aliens stayed in the jungle and waited until the time was right to fight their rivals in New York City.

The reptilians were treated as Gods and they painted the Amazonian snake aliens as devils and had the story of Eve in the Bible forever making the snake tainted in the eyes of the humans.

Centuries would pass and the reptilians enjoyed the dominance of being gods on Earth, but the Amazonians snake aliens had been hard at work. Snakes, whether earthly or alien, are patient creatures.

In 1977, they asserted power in New York City to show they were no longer the devils they had been painted as, in every book published by the reptilians.

I was a horny freshman at Columbia College in 1977. I knew I was gay and I found safety in the closet, but I'd sneak out of it from time to time to find a sexy bear down in Long Island.

I was and still am a twink, and the bears always loved me because of it.

I was not a twink by choice and could care less about working out. I love good greasy food as much as hairy big bears. My mom was so concerned about how skinny I was she had me see a doctor as a young boy. He told me I was born with a metabolism of a seven-foot tall 350 man, but I only grew to 5'4 and 100 pounds.

After a few times in the gay bars, I learned I was a bottom and was turned on by big tall bears. They made me feel safe, and safety felt sexy.

I'd take the train from Penn Station to Long Island and find the hairy guido bears from Hempstead. The gay guys down in Long Island were not very smart and didn't read much, (which I now realize was unintentionally very smart) but they were sweet and had a charm and realness that the queens in midtown lacked.

The night of the blackout I went to a gay Jets bar. I hated football, but I was a bears fan in many ways.

I ordered a screwdriver and sat there looking cute at the bar. I waited for the bears to notice me and come over and flirt, but they were too busy talking about Broadway Joe. Only in a bear bar in Long Island would a bunch of gay men talk about Joe Namath's quarterback skills instead of that cute ass of his. My dad didn't think much about me having a Namath quarterback picture in my room. He loved Broadway Joe. That poster had gotten me through some tough nights.

I felt annoyed hearing about how Namath wasn't the man he was when he won the Super Bowl, but a large man sat down next to me, lit up a cigarette, and in a gritty masculine voice I heard, "I fucking hate football, it reminds me of the war."

I could smell his sexy scent and I spotted his thick beard from the corner of my eye and I asked, "Do you have an extra smoke?"

"For you beautiful, of course."

He lit up my cigarette and said, "You're so young. Shit. I could tell you things that would make the pubes still growing on your cock fall off."

"I'm not going anywhere," I said and exhaled and I gave the smile I give all the bears before they decide to shove their cock in my mouth. I looked him right in his eyes. He was hot. Big, tall, and burly.

"We can't talk publicly, let's go in the bathroom, to the stall."

"Are we really going to talk?" I told him and winked.

"I am. You'll listen while you have my big dick in your mouth."

"I'm a good listener."

The bathroom was empty and much cleaner than the bar. Back in those days no one ever pissed or shit in the gay bar bathrooms; instead, we'd shit and piss in the alleys and fuck in the stalls.

His cock was out and I was in awe of it. It matched his big body. The dim light shined off the large throbbing head. I took it in my hands and spit on it. I stroked what barely fit in my hands. The spit was gone and the bathroom light reflected off his bulging dick head into my eyes.

He caressed my face and said, "Your eyes look so beautiful in the bathroom light. You still got your innocence. Go and take that cock, and I'll tell you something that will blow you away."

I nodded and opened my mouth like I was eating the new double pounders from McDonald's. My mouth was stuffed. So big. I loved the full feeling in my mouth that a huge cock gave me. I wasn't able to take all of him and I fondled his balls and sucked down to where his pubes touched my chin.

I sucked faster, he twirled my hair, and said, "I like you young twink boys, you remind me of a time when I was happy and innocent ... come on now, suck that dick, suck that cock like it's the last big juicy cock you might ever suck."

"oooh cccaaaayyy."

"Good. I know you get guys who tell you a lot about Nam, but they don't really know. They don't know why the war happened. Communism. Capitalism. Freedom. God. Race. It doesn't mean anything to them. We are just pawns to ... them."

"Bleeewhooooh?" I asked with his cock down my throat.

"In Nam, I saw them. I'll never forget that day. Never. Nope. Never. They were standing as tall as me but they weren't human. I was the only survivor of my unit; I was hiding in the bushes and saw their skin suits had been burnt off and both sides were looking at each other. Lizard people and snake men, staring each other down."

"Bwalaaaht," I said and spit out his cock.

"Keep sucking and listen, I don't care if you believe it or not. I have to tell people or I'll go as crazy as you think I sound."

He had PSTD, at least that was what I thought. I felt bad for him and wanted to make him feel better. What a waste of a lovely cock, though, but he had served what I thought was our country—he deserved a good cock sucking.

I took him back in my mouth and he continued, "The reptilians looked stronger. They outnumbered the snake people and they said, 'You think your new technology of the Internet can stop us. Fools! You snake aliens think you can slither around the world with your wires. Ha! We are in New York City, and our cum controls these Earthly monkey men. We've left our seed in so many humans to do our biddings. We control them, while you only slither aimlessly like you did in the story of Eve. We both fell to Earth from space, but we have ruled this land from day one and we will always rule it.'

The snakes hissed at him and responded also in unison, 'You're the fools! This was all a distraction, we have found our way onto the shores of Seattle and San Francisco, where we are protected in what will be called Silicon Valley. We will conquer you there and soon all of America and then the world. You fools taking your troops here to wipe out a rebellion. Ha, it will take time but by the time the Twenty First Century comes we will finally rule you. Snakes will control the wires, and the wires will make the world flat.'

The reptilians had heard enough and they killed all the snake aliens. Then they took out their lizard dicks and fucked their corpses; not out of lust but out of dominance. The reptilians I saw were necrophiliacs. Sex for them was not about pleasure but control.

I waited for them to cum on me and make me one of their cum slaves, but they never did. They didn't smell my fear and they left the dead snake aliens full of their magic cum ... I've never been the same since, it's been almost 7 years. I almost forgot about it ... like maybe it was a fever dream until I saw the snake eyes on the subway and the eyes of the Reptilians staring back at them on the way here."

He came hard in my mouth and I swallowed it down. It tasted good but this talk of reptile aliens in Vietnam made me nauseous and scared. It sounded so real to him and I don't why but I believed him. He wasn't a liar. I could always taste a man's character in his cum. This sexy bear was not crazy nor was he one of the method actors I would meet down in the Village. No, this was a man who had seen something and had lived to tell the tale.

We walked out of the bathroom and back into the gay bar. This was normally when I'd leave, but I was scared and wanted a man like him near me. I didn't want to stay at the stupid Football bar but I didn't want to leave him either. "You want to get out of here?" I asked.

He lit up a cigarette and said, "Fine, but wherever we go could be where we spend our last moments alive. I wanted a drink and a good cock sucking and I got that. So you choose, alright beautiful. Tell me where to go before the reptilian and snake war begins."

"The beach," I told him and felt less worried about the reptiles and hoped there'd be no sharks when we skinny-dipped. Jaws had still left me scared of the water.

"Ok, maybe the alien reptilians will be afraid of the ocean. All I know is something bad is going happen tonight."

His paranoia of aliens was annoying but mostly because it felt real. I tried not to focus on the alien talk and remembered how hot he was and how nice it would feel to take a skinny dip in the ocean. I also still needed to get off. "Let's head outside, the beach isn't far at all."

We left the bar and walked toward the beach when the lights went off.

All of New York City went black. We saw red and green eyes everywhere. They weren't human.

"Fuck, it's the reptilians and snake aliens! Run!"

Their eyes looked like bugs flying in the air but it didn't take long to see another color in the air—neon green—it was a flying liquid. I realized right away that it was reptilian cum.

"Shit, they are already ejaculating. They are going to bukkake all over the city, don't let their cum get in your mouth ..."

But it was too late, the reptilian cum and the blood of the snake people had already covered our bodies.

I was expecting to change and become their sex slave, but it only made me full for a moment; like my own needs for food were all taken away and I needed something to tell me what to do, but then my metabolism kicked in and my normal appetite came back.

My bear acted differently and so did the others. Sex acts spread through the city while reptilian aliens watched with their beady green eyes. My bear followed them, grabbed me, and bent me over. I saw other couples 69ing, fucking, and sucking.

The New York streets were becoming an orgy drenched in reptilian cum and soon human cum would flow as well.

The bear shoved his face in my ass and started tossing my salad. It felt so good, almost too good. It was mechanical. Like the bear was being mind controlled to perform the most perfect ass licking that was humanly possible.

As good of an ass licking it was, it was still missing something—the feel of a human touch. It was mechanical ass munching and it was not him doing it out of lust, but it was the reptilians trying to control me through a galactic rim job.

I was the only one there who wanted to stop the licking, fucking, and sucking. I broke away and began running towards the beach.

Alone in the blackness I ran. The neon cum kept exploding in the air like firecrackers of alien ejaculate. The moans of the reptilian sex slaves became louder but I heard hisses from the sea.

I reached the shore and saw great whale serpents.

They beached themselves onto shore. They stared at me with the same red snake eyes and spoke in unison, "You have their seed in you but you are not their pawn. You are the human of the prophecy of our people. Get in one of our mouths. We will not eat you, we will take you to safety."

"What am I, Jonas?"

"The reptilians wrote the Bible, us Amazon snakes are not devils. Do not believe their lies. Come to our new home in Seattle."

Like the story of Jonas I stayed inside of the belly of the alien snake whale for days. I survived off its alien body meat, which was full of food and holes. It even let me have sex with it. The body of the snake people aliens was euphoric. Where the reptilians would control you with sex, the snake aliens calmed you and took you to ecstasy with their bodies.

When we arrived, the whale snake spit me out and shape shifted into normal looking humans, but I could still tell who they were by their eyes.

We had reached the shores of Seattle and they said in unison, "Follow us to our castle to learn the truth."

I did and I saw what looked much more like a warehouse than a castle. I followed them inside where the snake people aliens were busy at work. They were building not only computers but all kinds of items that every American needs.

A snake man with a shaved head said, "You can call me by my human name; Jeff Bezos. We snake people believe that with our wire technology we can control the humans via their wants and needs. In time we will even be able to get the stories to you that you humans crave through the wires, paper will be burned and the wires will be like us and be able to slither everywhere. The new century is coming and we will take the power we have always deserved. Amazon will rule! Those who control not how to tell the story, but how the story is shared will have the power. The reptilians will soon feel our wrath and man will feel our power."

"Jeff, what ... ever the hell your name is ... just a few days ago I was blowing a gay bear Vietnam vet in a bathroom and he was telling me about you and the reptilians. He was really telling the truth. But... but..."

"You are immune to their cum like us. You are the only human we have encountered who did not become their cum puppet. The reptilians have gone from planet to planet cumming on anything. We Amazonians are a peaceful group. We only want to make and give people the best of things. The reptilians want to take, cum on all, and conquer. You are our prophet and we must now worship you in the only way we know how."

The snake aliens shed their skin off once again and all the worker snake men and women stopped their jobs but let the wires in the walls go into their scales. Each wire connected to another snake alien until they were all one and Jeff Bezos was the head snake and said, "We must make love. It is in the prophecy that the leader and the human must be one for the prophecy to finally happen."

He caressed my cheek and I felt the energy of all their bodies flow through mine. It was even better than the rim job the reptilians had the bear give me. He ripped off my clothes and all the snakes began to hiss, not with anger, but with lust.

He rubbed my little pecs and pinched my hard nipples. The bears never took the time to appreciate my body, they just wanted to bend me over and get to it, but Jeff, the snake alien leader made sure to feel all of me.

His scaled hands had a sense of touch that showed me that my human body had only felt a small percentage of what pleasure really could be, but Jeff wasn't done. His penis shot around and like a snake. It expanded for the attack and went right into my anus. I had experienced a few cocks in my ass, and some felt better than others, but this was heaven.

I could feel every thought, emotion, and sensation of all the snake aliens in my asshole.

He thrusted more and harder and all the memories and desires of the snake people became mine. I saw how they wanted revenge on the reptilians, how they were sick of being the weaker ones on this planet, how they wanted to tell their story to the humans.

The snake alien came in my ass and past, present, and future were no more. There was only singularity. The digitality and I were one.

I could tell you about the snake alien orgies for all the years I lived and worked for Amazon. How the centuries passed, as we worked and fucked, until our empire became the biggest seller of books and products.

The fucking and the wires gave us motivation and strength through the years. Our sexuality was not used for control, but for inspiration. The west coast became a hot spot snake for web activity; from Silicon Valley to Seattle we were finding ways to take on the reptilians in New York City.

It all changed when King Jeff came up with the Kindle. It not only took away influence of the reptilians of New York City, but it took their actual power away.

The reptilians were only able keep their power and magic through wood.

The planet that the reptilians had come from had no electricity; only water, wood, and their neon cum. The lived off all three and harnessed their own powers through those resources. They evolved to put their psychic energy into the paper they'd scape off the trees. Not only was their neon cum very special, but anything they put onto paper was as well.

It was different for the snake people; their original planet had electromagnetism and wiring. They were the opposite of the reptilians and were actually weakened by trees. When they fell to earth and landed in the rainforest of the Amazon, they were left weakened and desolate while the reptilians were strengthened.

The power has shifted in favor of the snake people. The Kindle has gained ground as you, yes you, are reading this in your hand or even on your IPAD right now.

I have chosen to go through Mandy De Sandra and to put this story under the erotica genre in order to give you the whole unedited truth.

I wish the orgy was the only the stuff that happened with the snake people, but I see now that the snake aliens are just as bad, only in different ways. They tried to brainwash me with their hot sex. I sucked off every big snake cock that existed, but soon my lust grew flaccid and I saw him or her for what they really were: Evil overlords waiting to rule Earth.

The reptilians and the snake people do not care about us. They only treated me kindly because they thought I was their prophet but the truth is they hate humans as much as the reptilians do. The snake people also want a world were stories do not matter. Stories are just a way for the snakes to keep tabs on us, no different than the other products that are gathered in Seattle and sent around the world.

The war has started and I left the snake people and I am now non-aligned to either side.

I only understand in my old age, that there is no way to conquer the reptilians or the Amazonian snake people.

The only way for us humans to win is to let them kill each other.

Old age brings clarity and I always thought the cum didn't turn me into a sex slave because of my metabolism, but that was not the case.

It was so simple but I didn't realize until I read a PDF of *City on Fire* and got bored because it was too damn long.

Reading that way too fucking long and pretentious book I saw I was unaffected by the reptilians and by the lies of *City On Fire*, because I already knew the story of the reptilians and the Amazonian snakes.

When I sucked off the bear in the bathroom and he told me the story, the reptilian psychic energy had no control over me. To know the existence of their psychic energy is to make it powerless.

With this e-book, you now know the same.

A story is something human and primal that doesn't come from aliens but from the darkest and brightest parts of men and women's souls. This story is always yours and anything that is alien and powerful, becomes familiar and weak when you know its truth.

You must share this with all your friends in order to break the alien reptilian and snake Amazonian mind control over the human race.

We must enjoy their stories, whether they are from reptilians or Amazonian snakes, they are still from man and from the soul. The minute we forget that, they will always beat us.

God Speed,

Survivor of the 77 Bukkake Blackout, Kilgore Troutdale

The Haunting of the Paranormal Romance Awards

It was the moment they had all been waiting for at RomCom: who would win the Haunted Heart Award for Best Paranormal Romance Novel. The competition was stiff involving *Angels in Chains* by Cynthia Eden, *Immortally Yours* by Angie Fox, *Mark of the Witch* by Maggie Shayne, and *My Husband Never Left* by newcomer Shira Constantine.

The Husband Who Never Left was different than the other novels, while they had their typical plots of vampires, spirits, and angels who fell for a fictional female protagonists, Shira saw her novel as a memoir, though her editor and psychiatrist felt it would be better if they presented it as fiction.

But it was real to Shira.

She wrote with passion and honesty about how her dead husband loved her so much that he haunted her home and ravished her at night while other lonely ghosts and spirits watched.

It was a touching, if not slightly kinky love story that many housewives enjoyed. While her book had the same amount of melodrama and lackluster style of writing as the other romances, her book stuck out—it felt real.

It also had a more literary quality: the ending was not the typical 'they lived happily ever after.' Instead it left you wondering how her husband and his lost spirit friends could enter the living world as one being.

Many assumed it would be series.

The rest of the paranormal romance writers found the book and her strange (and her outfit, because she looked like a mourning lunch lady), yet the story was special and so it was making more waves on Twitter and chatrooms than all the other books combined. There was an animosity toward Shira from the other writers because in their own haunted hearts they knew Shira wrote the best book—even if was really weird.

Shira believed this too and she was told by her spirit husband that if she won this award then the spirit world would let him and the other ghosts finally become real. She wanted this more than anything. She sat and waited as the other paranormal romance writers sipped their martinis and wine glasses in the dining room.

They were all sipping their fancy drinks as the hunk and host Fabio took the mike, "Aw, yea everybody, we having such good time; so many nice prizes for so many nice books. Our next award I can relate to cause I'm old I am getting so close to death, ah-ha-ha-ha. But I still have great hair. The award is for Best Paranormal Romance Novel of the year and our special guest and presenter Amanda Hocking. Aw, she so beautiful."

Amanda was wearing a casual white t-shirt that said "I Suck" with a few blood drops along with a black pantsuit. Fabio gave her the stage and most of the women in the audience turned their full attention upon him. Even when they were little girls they snuck books with him on the covers finding a magical world that most of their husbands could not provide when they became adults.

Amanda cleared her throat and the women looked at her with envy and awe, "Hello, it is so cool to be here. As last year's winner, I am very excited to hand over the torch of being totally cool in the spirit world."

The audience all laughed except the nominees, they were all balls of nerves. The event was being live Tweeted and the winner would get a big boost in their Amazon sales.

Amanda read the names and there was the standard clap until she called out Sharia's name and the name of her book. The crowd gave a half-hearted clap as Sharia talked to her dead husband (which is not appropriate to do even at the Paranormal Romance Awards), "Our love and your restless soul will be consummated with this award. It will free you and our love will have a tangible outlet and we will finally feel true bliss and peace."

All the Romance writers could her and they thought she really was weird. Sure, they *marketed* themselves as weird but that was because many of their publicists wanted to make sure they got the *Hot Topic* crowd, since they had more money to spend than even the housewives.

Sharia began saying a strange Vodooesque Wiccan prayer. Amanda and the others tried to pretend that she wasn't there as Amanda Hocking called out the nominees.

Shia stopped praying the moment that Amanda Hocking said, "And our winner for best paranormal romance novel...oh, it was my favorite too. *Immortally Yours* by Angie Fox."

There were loud claps as a smiling Fox walked to the stage to receive the award but Shira was full of rage. She stormed up onto the stage and took the award from Hocking.

One of the losers, Cynthia Eden said, "She's pulling a Paranormanye."

"What's that?" Asked other loser, Maggie Shayne.

"Like what Kanye did with Taylor Swift but for Paranormal Romance." Eden replied.

She and the other women sitting the audience gasped when Shira held the award up like Moses and pushed Angie Fox aside. The golden award of a black and gold heart reflected all the shocked faces in the crowd on its shining surface.

Shia didn't care and said, "Look at all of you, thinking you know love and the dark side; writing books that lack art and humanity, just preying on the fears and desires of the lonely. You have no sense of what art is and no sense of the truth. I live a paranormal romance. You think writing about spirits and love has no consequences. You think this is just all fun and games. It's not! My husband is a real ghost and my real love is here and he is angry and so are his friends. Making money off their suffering, telling stories for fun; those are the true horrors. And worse; not rewarding mine: my story of truth of art. You not only rejected me, you rejected honoring the sprits. Now you can answer to them."

The dining room doors slammed closed and the lights dimmed. Shira laughed as thunder vibrated off the wine and martini glasses. The women were petrified; the sprits started to howl like a scene out of many of their novels.

The award in Shira's hand started to turn red and blood dripped down until the golden heart broke and angry ghoulish spirits flew out.

Many of the stories of paranormal romance that these women wrote were about the spirits needing a human hearts to feel alive—this was half true.

The spirits needed hearts because eating and living inside them gave them more power.

Shira watched all the spirits fly around the giant banquet hall.

She screamed to them, "Take their hearts, they don't deserve them."

Amanda Hocking ducked in fright and screamed, but a black spirit resembling Death went down her throat and ripped her beating heart out. The other spirits did the same and all the other A to F-List romantic writers had all their hearts ripped out and taken by the spirits as well.

There were paranormal novelist causalities everywhere as the spirits went through their mouths and noses to take their hearts to a spot where they piled them all up into the shape of human being.

The still beating hearts of the romantic novelists was merging into one being.

Each spirit went inside one heart and became one single body of hearts.

They walked toward Shira.

She smiled, happy to finally be at one with her husband. She went to kiss the head of the body of hearts but her skin was ripped off and became the skin of the heart body.

In shock and pain Sharia screamed, "Why? I loved all of you."

"We love skin."

"But my husband."

"He is in heaven. We are not and we need skin." The heart body answered back as all of Shia's skin was ripped off her bones to cover the heart body.

Shira died on the spot looking at the bald heart body of spirits that had deceived her.

All the romance writers were dead, some in heaven, some in hell.

The only person still alive was Fabio who was shaking violently and hiding under a chair.

The heart body walked toward him; it looked down and told Fabio, "I like your hair."

The Infinite Jest of Picking Porn Titles (Featuring C. Paul)

My job at the porn store in SE DC where I worked for many years while I got an MA in Creative Writing was as varied and diverse as our clientele. Every Tuesday at 3:00 PM I would get an e-mail with a list of new porn titles available for purchase; my job was to review this list and pick the titles we would carry and include in our new release order.

I based my choices on the title, brand, and what I felt was best for our customers which was predominately based on my observations of said clientele: 80% older African-American/African, 15% Hispanic, 3% lesbians, and a few old white guys who thought the internet had spies and/or communist rogues.

Making this decision was tough but using a process that includes my liberal arts education with a strong focus on the humanities I was able to make winning picks with only the The Brand, Theme, and Title. I backed my porn choices by citing sources that included footnotes at the bottom of the page in the form of a bibliography.

As every Tuesday I channeled the great thinker David Foster Wallace where Tuesday at 3:00 PM became known as the Infinite Jest of Picking Porn Titles:

HOME MADE—MASTURBATION "SOLO MASTURBATION #12"

I always pass on solo masturbation movies. Men do not enjoy watching them; I think psychologically it plays on the male fear of being replaced and unneeded#1. More importantly aesthetically my customers do not enjoy solo masturbation, as one of our loyal customers Leroy#2 an African-American in his mid 60's shared his thoughts on solo masturbation films, "I wanna see a dick up that girl, not some rubber; bitch ain't driving a car, she riding a dick." Touché' Leroy, touché.

TREASURE ISLAND—GAY "IN THE FLESH"

I needed to include gay titles but it helps if it involves African-American men who are in the closet, our best-selling title is "Secrets in Da Hood."#3 The plots many times show gangstas#4 after they have committed a drive-by who then console each other with their penises or they go to each other 'cause "the hoodrats#5 just don't understand what a mother fucker needs". These are the plots, as the covers usually show alpha male black men wearing bandanas staring at each other with a look of longing in their eyes. A definite yes.

CHANNEL 69—OLDER "MATURE WOMEN # 73"

Though I need to pick a MILF title, and the movie below is a hairy genre which is also needed in the selection, but the brand Channel 69 is very poor quality and by quality I will use the term used in "Zen and The Art of Motorcycle Maintenance",#6 which states 'quality' has classical attributes (good camera work, attractive women, tight editing) and romantic attributes (emotional performances, believable cock craving, and I guess what the French would call 'Je ne sais quoi' that thing you can't classify but you like it) The Channel 69 brand lacks neither and I would not purchase it for my customers.

CHANNEL 69—HAIRY "FRESH AND HAIRY # 2"

I try to get at least 1 hairy but Channel 69 is a no go. To add to the statement above I will quote one of our regulars Ralph,#7 "Nuttin ever good on channel 69 son; I turn that mother fucker off."

HEAT WAVE—BLACK "BBBW # 34"

This film would not be taken because the brand 'Heat Wave' has received many complaints: 'sloppy girls and sloppy camera work'. I had one customer even complain that the 'Heat Wave Hoes' had ass implants#8 and he could tell this because 'they don't bounce right, it ain't right'. So for quality#9 sake I would refrain from getting the brand 'Heat Wave'.

WHITE GHETTO—SHEMALE "MY GIRLFRIENDS GIANT COCK # 8"

I will have to get at least one shemale video. Though this is a good title; one of our most popular tranny series is Transsexual Prostitutes.#10 I once received a call once from a concerned customer's wife worried that her husband might actually be seeing transsexual prostitutes. I calmed her down and said that this is a fad and men only watch these videos but do not act on them. She cried a little and said something in Spanish.#11 I felt bad for her and tried to comfort her saying, "It is very popular in the Hispanic community, but I don't know why." She then said she married a maracone#12, and hung up. I am not sure why but the predominant customers who rent tranny movies are hispanic men, who I assume to be in the closet. I asked this hot Hispanic girl#13 who cooks hamburgers at my favorite establishment The Korzo Haus#14 why this was and she said it was because no one is thought to be gay in the Hispanic community and if anyone asks he could say it wasn't that "Maricones" because she had boobs. That aside, a big penis on big breasts is always a good transsexual movie. I will select this one unless "Tranny Prostitutes 74" is available.

ABIGAIL—LESBIAN "LONDON KEYES"

The actress London Keys#15 is a quite possible lock; she is a special combination of an Orientalist#16 Fetish, an hour-glass figure, with a generous backside. She is also a fan of anallingus#17 which can be appreciated in the porn renting community. Though these are all positive attributes, the African-American majority does not care for lesbian videos#18 and she does not fit the Caucasian orientalist fetish; I would have to pass on Mrs. Keyes–though I appreciate her style and sexual proclivity; it is not about the writer–it is about the customer. Also the brand Abigail sounds artsy and like art films, art porn is not appreciated by the general porn public. In the end people want of see Transformers over The Tree of Life.#19

CHEATERS CLUB—CUCKOLD "CHEATING WIVES # 24"

Cuckold movies#20 do very well, there is a surprising amount of white men that come in and buy these videos. They usually look like accountants or the managers you would see at Bennigans who never excelled in sports like Dodgeball. There are some interesting theories about why many men would be into watching or getting cuckold–Evolutionary, male to male competition or what Dr. Robin baker coined the term 'Sperm Wars'#21 has played a role in reproductive stagey. The theory is that we could be programmed to be turned on by infidelity to make sure to produce other fighter sperm. This also plays into the idea of concealed ovulation and women liking certain types of men when ovulating#22. Or it could just be the decadent times we live. There are no easy answers to this phenomenon but until it gets figured out the writer would look for covers of dorky guys looking upset while their wife is being banged by a big penis stud.

HUSTLER–SHEMALE "SHEMALE SUPERSTARS # 7"

This would be the second shemale pick unless 'Tranny Prostitutes 74' is available. The 'Shemale Superstars Series' has very much tricked the writer. Every time the writer looked down at the face on the cover and found the woman very attractive and then looked lower and enjoyed the breasts, and then went lower to check out the vaginal area the writer saw a very large penis#23 being tricked every time. These men have such attractive feminine faces that it fools everyone who looks. Another popular title is 'Tranny Surprise', if that or 'Tranny Prostitutes' are not available then I will select these two tranny films and will continue to look too low when it comes to tranny covers; it is very much porn store 'Ground Hog Day'#24

POWERSVILLE—CUM SHOTS "COLLEGE SPUNKFEST"

Now the owner suggested we get one blow job film but we officially call them facials. Our customers would refer to them as 'Head Joints.'#25 If you look on the back cover you will usually see a young girl who looks like Elmer's glue fell on her face. The philosophy & symbolism of the facial is quite a novelty and could appeal to the sense of power: I have so many sexual options instead of leaving my semen in your vagina for reproductive purposes I will leave it on your face. On a side note the image I've seen for this certain sexual practice will always be a girl at a beauty salon getting ready for a facial (the one of beautification purposes) looking in a mirror and see a large cock with sperm coming out toward her face. Not sure if it a lack of creativity or if this the best way to advertise for the genre#26?

CABALLERO—GAY "THE 300"

Now this would be a good pick for gay men of all colors. The title would suggest the men would be rather buff, have good-sized penises, and I noticed gay men want a minor story they can watch after eating a good meal or after they have watched a design show on Bravo#27

EVIL—ANAL "OCCUPYMYASS (2 DISC SET)"

It is important to buy anal, the 'Evil' series had a very good reputation of being the Spielberg of butt sex. A good political pun is also a plus because the shop is in DC and my customers no matter what their level of education can appreciate a politically charged pun or movie—it is a sense of DC pride—though the "Obama Bangs Your Mama"#28 series did not do so well or did 'Cash for Chunkers'#29 which had an Obama look-a-like on the cover giving money to larger women but the one film where an Obama look-a-like banged a Sarah Palin look-alike Lisa Ann#30 was a best rental and seller.

JULES JORDAN—INTERRACIAL "PHAT ASS WHITE BOOTY # 7"

This what we call a 'triple hit'#31 and I would be tempted to buy 2 copies. Good brand, good title, series, & interracial. The brothas that shop the store are definitely fans of the large booty and though caucasian men do not prefer a good-sized booty, scientifically a big booty is much healthier because an hour-glass figure and a generous backside means high fertility rate and less chance of getting diabetes#32...it could be that I worked at the porn store for so long, but the writer though of southern Italian descent is also big booty lover. Sir Mix A Lot#33 knew what was up.

BRAZZERS—BIG TITS "BIG TITS AT WORK #15"

Brazzers is a great brand; it is cover model looking women with fake breasts wanting penises. The brand is very much a standard and echo of society's views of female beauty and Brazzers caters to this standard of beauty along with men with money. It is rich old men that don't want their trophy wives to see porn on their computers that buy these titles, the brothas stay away from them while middle class white men usually use the internet. Brazzers is the most conscious use of class and economic disparity and from a Marxist#34 view Brazzers would be propagating the bourgeoise view that beauty is a product and big titties are stopping the proletariat revolution#35...or it could be, some people just like big fake titties.

BEAR FILMS—GAY "STOGLE BEARS"

Bear films are specific gay genre which involves hairy large men. This genre very much goes against the Apollonian Beauty#36 of men that echoes back from ancient Greece#37. These are men you would imagine as lumberjacks or related to the producer character in 'Borat'.#38 I do get older queens who stay in Dupont Circle who like to come to the store slumming looking to buy poppers#39 and will buy films like a Bear Film or two—one stylish homosexual while purchasing a Bear Film told me that poppers numb and stretch out the anus and make things rock hard. I said that sounds pretty cool and told him to enjoy his poppers and movie...the writer wanted to quote Yogi Bear but remained professional.

ELEGANT ANGEL —SQUIRTING "REAL FEMALE ORGASMS # 15"

This is a good brand and I do need a squirt title. We have a section just for squirting#40 and the squirt fans usually buy squirt movies in bulk. The writer will now put himself out on a limb and label squirting videos one of the healthiest forms of 3rd Wave feminism#41 in porn. It is a very powerful image of empowerment and equality of a man getting a squirt facial. The idea of a woman doing a sexual act on a man that a man usually does to degrade women is very poetic and shows that we are closer to equality–unfortunately though there are now cheesy new age guys#42 taking advantage of this desire to teach techniques so their 'yin lovers' can squirt. I do not know if these techniques can work, but the writer will take a stand stating that squirting could be a way to stop the battle of the sexes#43

3RD DEGREE — GANGBANG "MY FIRST GANG BANG # 2"

How can there be two firsts? Porn titles do not really worry about logical thinking and can be very much reflection of zen koans#44. The gangbang is another novelty, that goes back to our more primal days of sexual competition of sperm wars. There is also pagan feel to them, as the book Sexual Personae#45 argues the paganism stamped out by Christian Tradition tries to find its way in pornography. Many male customers have been very staunchly anti-gangbang but I would argue that the act of gangbanging plays to the male fantasy ideal: guaranteed sex while hanging out with their friends–there are as many high fives as there are penises in gangbang movies.#46

COMBAT ZONE — INTERRACIAL "MOMMY ME AND A GANGSTER"

A good title will have me be able to pick the cover. There will be a 37-year-old blond and a black man wearing gold teeth, a hoodie, chain, and or a t-shirt that says 'I own dat pussy'. The story lines will be something along the lines of he is a drug dealer and needs to hide out and she has never been with a black man before and he takes out his gun but she can still see the package through his baggy pants.#47 Banging begins. A Keeper.

HUSH HUSH—WHITE "MASSIVE"

I would only get this if it stared the porn star Whitezilla#48—he is quite a talent and is even respected by black customers. He is the Larry Bird of porn and as helped promote (purposely or not) racial integration as there was a nice porn moment when Whitezillia and Blackzilla teamed up for a series on a mission to 'stretch out the sluts'. Though stretching out sluts is not a feminist activity, we must pick our battles in this world injustice and prejudice and at least two men of different skin color sharing their God-Given talents to achieve a goal together is progressive.#49

EVASIVE—BLACK "DRIPPING WET BLACK ASSES # 2"

Now Evasive was a good brand, many of the older brothas would always request it. Usually anything that involves the words 'drip, wet, black, asses' I will probably take; porn titles in the end very much reflect google#50 searches. This is the era we live in where it will not be about sentences or titles but about details. Even disenchantment#51can find its way to pornography.

ACTIVE DUTY—GAY "BATTLE CRY THE TRILOGY"

Now this sounds like an excellent gay film. Every once in a while an ambitious director comes out and says "Hey, yes I am making a porno, yes penises will be going into anuses but it can still have a story#52 it can still be art." If it was just a regular straight porn film, the writer wouldn't even give it a second look but this is something slumming Du Pont gays would buy while picking up their poppers. So I would add this to the list. I can picture a touching scene when two men come to terms with death & love and then you know blow each other.

VOUYER 4 HRS—BIG BUTT "BIG ASS SLUTS"

If it has the word big ass in the title; the writer will buy it for his customers and my might even watch it when not writing or watching ESPN#53 or the Gilmore Girls.#54 It is also a good financial choice as any brans with 4 hours on it is a mix not a new release and therefore cheaper. We should sill charge it as a new release so I made sure to get at least 1 big booty titles that is the 4 hour mix compilations.

Bibliography

1.   The New York Times columnist Maureen Dowd wrote a book "Are Men Necessary". It is provocative question because there is some validity to question. Even misogynistic lothario character Roger Dodger an early 2000 film of the same title argues that once women figures out telepathy we will be pretty worthless, except for our sperm. I apologize gentleman to start this bibliography on such a sour note.

2.   Leroy liked to gamble and always paid in quarters. He was old school and liked the Red Skins and "hoes that can keep quiet by having my dick in their

mouth—all day." Leroy was single for all 2 years I worked there and though he had character issues he could always make change for the writer and he is appreciated to this day for his change and interesting opinions.

3.   This would make for a good documentary: Gay Gangbangaz. One of the most riveting and interesting characters of this new century was Omar Little of the HBO Show 'The Wire'.

4.   A term originated from the west coast hip hop scene. The music in these films usually echo early 90's hip hop like West Side Connection. It could be west coast bias as most porn movies are shot in the valley. But I am sure brothas in Harlem & the Bronx have secrets in their hood as well. RIP Tupac & Biggie

5.   A negative term for straight females who have high sexual proclivity and lack high character and self-esteem. Not to be confused with a chickenhead who are just hoes who lack the funds to get their hair done.

6.   Zen and The Art of Motorcycle Maintenance was a book written by man who had a mental breakdown & went on a motorcycle trip with his son on a quest to find out the definition of quality that would also become a spiritual guide for men that are divorced in their 40's.

7.   Ralph was an old school black man that lived near the porn store. He usually had a frown on his face complaining about a movie's lack of quality. Ralph was the unofficial porn critic of the store. The only film the writer ever saw him say anything positive about was "Big Ass Stalker".

8.   There is philosophical code with some men who believe that a women should be natural (make up, weaves, shaving, & push up bras are ok) but foreign objects inserted into the body are not in good taste. Ass implants was too much for men that are titty & booty naturalists. Though the writer can go with or without big fake titties, the writer looked himself at the Heat Wave video and saw it was true: girls with ass implants—they just don't bounce right.

9.   The writer feels strongly that 'Zen and The Art of Motorcycle Maintenance' is a very good philosophical book. Its biggest strength besides its definition of quality is exploring the two rival belief systems: classical & romantic echo another great work of philosophy 'The Birth of Tragedy' by Frederick Nietzsch The writer is not sure why this specific brand of tranny movies is so popular. I guess these men were finding

constructive ways to live out a fantasy they could not act out on.

10.   Not sure but I believe the word gonyo was used which means fuck.

11.   Homosexual in spanish.

12.   I have a good friendship with this hot chica. I eat at The Korzo Haus and we talk a lot & laugh. The friendship is very much like Luke and Lorelai from the enjoyable show 'The Gilmore Girls' but I do not see a season 4 happening because the hamburger girl requires a 'baller' and I am a poor writer & musician but if this book or my band does well I will take her salsa dancing and to a fancy non-hamburger restaurant.

13.   My favorite eating establishment in the NYC area located on AVE B & East 7th st. My favorite's are Steven's Dream Balls and The Original.

14.   An attractive curvy Asian girl, who both myself and my drummer Baron Apollo would both enjoy having sex with.

15.   'Orientalism' is a book by Edward Said with the thesis: western white people had created myths for the middle east and the orient that has propagated unhealthy and many times non realistic stereotypes. Porn capitalizes on Orientalism propagating these

myths of the subservient Asian women and harems in the middle east.

16.   Licking someone's anus which is usually performed by the man on the woman but in the heat of the moment the woman can return the favor. The woman performing the rim job is usually considered a special act unless it is a speciality video like 'she licks ass.'

17.   The African-American community is not big supporters of lesbian videos. Ironically there are more forms of homophobia in the black community than the white community. Prop 8 was passed through the support of the African-American community. I would like to be an olive branch to the gay & African American Community and say that each other is not the enemy-prude uptight white people are-one love.

18.   A very overrated art film that involved home videos of Brad Pitt spliced with a PBS special about dinosaurs and Sean Penn reflecting on life after he learned Bush got reelected.

19.   Movies that involve married men having their wives cheat on them. It is usually against their will but they concede out of fear of their wife leaving them. These movies are nihilistic and racially charged usually

the dude she cheats with is either black, sometimes he his white, but the "Bull" always has a very large penis. These movies are pure Darwinism as women talk about getting impregnated by the bigger man. Yet there is always a twist in these movies as the cuckolds get very turned on by this. It could be a form of slave mentality to quote Nietzsche were the weaker finds meaning it "submissive behavior" or it could be the man lacks self-respect and self-esteem and plays out his insecurities in a Freudian sexual manner. The writer is not sure if we should feel sorrow or laugh at the cuckolded. Maybe both.

20.   The sperm war theory is a thesis by Robin Baker that states sperms are not just there to impregnate but that there are sperm born only to fight with another man's sperm. That in our more primal days women would copulate with multiple men and have a "sperm war". With the theory of Kamikaze sperm, it would make sense for men to be very turned on by another man sleeping with his mate so he could have fighter sperm protect the egg. Orgasm also leads to more sperm being absorbed so if he's not getting the job done he is at a disadvantage. Rousseau's idea of nature & the noble beast being benevolent falls short next to cuckold

movies. In the porn store Hobbes and De Sade win the battle of what it means to be human.

21.   It could be why human women evolved concealed ovulation. Cuckolding could be historical reproductive strategy. Yet, the writer does not want to promote such a negative view of humanity and believes that spiritual growth will be human beings out growing the negative behaviors of our caveman ancestors.

22.   The writer has looked at 38 tranny penises accidentally.

23.   An excellent movie by Bill Murray that all spiritual belief systems support for its living each day message. I wish I had figured out what Bill did but In the end i always see nice pair of tits and then a big dick.

24.   Head Joints is a slang term for oral sex that involves the female sucking the penis to climax. Though in real life the male preference is to have the sperm be swallowed but in porn it is preferred that the climax winds up on the woman's face.

25.   For now the porn industry keeps using salon's for facial covers. It could be the old saying: if ain't broke don't fix it.

26.   A television channel that features many design shows and the hit show 'The Millionaire Matchmaker'. I

would watch it at the store but many of the customers did not share the writers enthusiasm for the show. My theory for their hating is men on the lower economic scale are not going to root for a protagonist who should be "up in some bomb ass pussy after taking hoes to the Cheese Cake Factory."

27.   America is a patriotic country, even our perverts are patriotic. Though the covers are very amusing most men do not want to watch the president have sex. The black community very much has reverence for Obama. So his 'Obama Bangs Your Mama' series were not popular.

28.   "Cash for Chunkers" was political driven porn celebrating Keynesian economics and large women. The cover involved a Obama look a like giving dollar bills to a chubby blond woman. Though the writer shares a libertarian philosophy I must admit the cash for clunkers was moderately successful or maybe I am just comparing it to the "Cash for Chunkers" series which wasn't successful.

29.   Lisa Ann is the porn version to Tina Fey's Sarah Palin, the video was very popular of Obama having sex of with Sarah Palin because of the strong dislike of Palin

and the symbolism of Obama putting his penis his Sarah Palin's anus.

30.   A term used for a video that is guaranteed to sell.

31.   There have been studies to show it is healthy to have a big booty and even prevents diabetes. Many black man do not fall prey to society's standard of beauty and instead appreciate a girl with some curves and a good-sized gluttonous maximus. The writer shares the ideology of the booty and was coined by 6 black men at the porn store an 'honorary brotha'-word is bond.

32.   A great hip hop song celebrating the love of good-sized booties.

33.   Marxism would see Brazzers films of blocking the utopia of equality. Fake breasts are a form of capital controlling the minds of the working class from revolution. Though if Marx saw a Brazzers movie he might have just masturbated instead of writing the 'Communist Manifesto'.

34.   If we all had equal sized penises, butts, breasts, maybe the revolution would happen. But until then it is sexual desire that will stop Marxist Utopia.

35.   I am using the definition by Camile Pagilia used in the book 'Sexual Personae'.

36.   In Ancient Greece men slept with younger men and the beauty they preferred was skinny, feminine, hairless, and a small penis.

37.   For those who haven't seen the movie it is a man who is very hairy & overweight. The opposite of what is referred to as a twink: young, in shape, pretty boy.

38.   They are sniffed and are very popular with the gay community. The most popular brand was Locker Room.

39.   Squirting is quite a mystery. Some girls can squirt, some can't. The theory is that is it involves hitting the G Spot that leads to female ejaculation. The fluid is not urine but can be labeled 'lady love drops.'

40.   Though the writer very much supports the ideals of third wave feminism.

41.   'Ideagasms' squirt instructor video. The reader can google that one.

42.   The writer roots for equality and understanding from both sexes. Love is a choice of deciding to be equal with the other. If we can focus more on being equal and unless on power we might all have more fulfilling

relationships were squirting is not required but not denied.

43.   Zen religious word plays to bring you closer to not thinking and finding enlightenment.

44.   A very proactive book that argues pornography is art and paganism though not in religion anymore finds it ways in art or skin flicks. Though this is the writer's favorite non-fiction book, the writer did not share Pagilia's negative view on Lady Gaga-she is an Appolian revelation with a pop melody.

45.   There is never any competition with the boys it is usually cooperative and if there was not a girl with a penis in her mouth, anus, and vagina it would be a like a night at your neighborhood sports bar.

46.   The style of baggy pants originated in jail to try to not show their figure to male rapists.

47.   A rising star in the porn industry with a penis over 9 inches with coke can girth. He is the 21st century John Holmes.

48.   Though their goals are anti-feminist they do promote racial integration. In the goal of equality the writer sees race first, then sex, & finally sexual orientation.

49.   We do live in a time where we are led by our google searches where buzz words will lead us instead of quality.

50.   Disenchantment is prevalent in the modern age; it is a feeling lost in the modern secular world: it is something we fight but also accept.

51.   The best screen writing is gay male porn. The writer wrote one "On The Cock" and is very proud of the piece. He hopes it will be made one day in the film and it was featured on The Homo Sex Blog.

52.   See "Story: Substance, Structure, Style, and the Principles of Screenwriting" by Robert McKee.

53.   The writer watched 'First Take' in the morning & enjoyed the debates with Skip Bayless & Stephen A Smith while putting rented videos. The writer shares Skip's views of Tebow but not his Prince James Message.

54.   The writer watched every episode of The Gilmore Girls at the porn store on ABC Family. The brothas gave the writer much jabbing for being a 'pussy ass nigga' but the strength of the writing came through where many patrons of the porn store later agreed & got emotionally involved with two plots of the show "that little nigga Jess belongs with Rory, fuck that herb nigga

Dean." & also "that nigga Luke needs to man up and give Laurali the good dick. Them mother fuckers are in love. Niggas don't make special pancakes & shit unless she is his boo. For real." Their love was very real and the writer feels there should be a movie to show that love and wedding between Luke & Lorelai.

About The Author

Mandy De Sandra is alter-ego of Bizarro-YA author Christoph Paul. They can both be reached at Mandydesandra@gmail.com. If you enjoyed this book please leave a review and say hi to Mandy at Twitter @MandyDesandra. If you want read more Mandy De Sandra give "Ravished By Reagansaurus" a read. If you are curious about Bizarro Fiction go to Bizarrocentral.com.

CPSIA information can be obtained
at www.ICGtesting.com
Printed in the USA
FFOW03n2159071216
30190FF